"We're not going to have an affair, Jake."

Jake's mouth drifted across the line of Cassie's jaw to nibble at her earlobe. "We already are having an affair. We just haven't gotten as far as the bedroom yet."

"I see." Cassie tried to keep her voice light. "Well, that must explain why I don't recall sleeping with you. I thought surely it couldn't have just slipped my mind, but—"

"Oh, you'll remember it, all right," Jake said gruffly. "I'll guarantee it."

Hiring
Ms. Right

Three single women, one home-help agency—and three professional bachelors in need of...a wife?

*Are you a busy executive with a demanding career?

*Do you need help with those time-consuming everyday errands?

*Ever wished you could hire a house-sitter, caterer...or even a glamorous partner for that special social occasion?

Meet **Cassie, Sabrina** and **Paige**—three independent women who've formed a business taking care of those troublesome domestic crises.

And meet the three gorgeous bachelors who are simply looking for a little help...and instead discover they've hired Ms. Right!

Enjoy bestselling author **Leigh Michaels**'s new trilogy:

Husband on Demand—On sale April 2000
Bride on Loan—On sale May 2000
Wife on Approval—On sale June 2000

Husband
on Demand
Leigh Michaels

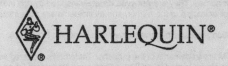

HARLEQUIN®

TORONTO • NEW YORK • LONDON
AMSTERDAM • PARIS • SYDNEY • HAMBURG
STOCKHOLM • ATHENS • TOKYO • MILAN • MADRID
PRAGUE • WARSAW • BUDAPEST • AUCKLAND

ISBN 0-373-03600-0

HUSBAND ON DEMAND

First North American Publication 2000.

Copyright © 2000 by Leigh Michaels.

CHAPTER ONE

THE key was right where Peggy always left it, under the pot of bright yellow mums beside the front door of the townhouse. But this time, instead of putting it back as soon as she'd unlocked the door, Cassie dropped the key into the pocket of her tweed jacket and bent to pick up her tote bag and suitcase.

Just inside the painfully silent foyer, with the door pushed closed behind her, she stopped to look around.

Which was silly, of course, for it wasn't as if she didn't know almost every inch of Peggy Abbott's house. Cassie couldn't count the times she'd been there, putting away the dry cleaning in the master-bedroom closets, or picking up a shopping list from Peggy's desk in the tiny study. Last Christmas she'd spent a whole day in the kitchen, wrapping gifts and baking cookies for the Abbotts' holiday open house.

Sometimes Peggy was there when Cassie stopped by, more often she wasn't. But this time was different. This time Cassie wasn't simply running an errand but actually moving in. And this time the townhouse seemed watchful and wary, instead of warm and welcoming.

Cassie shook her head a little and smiled at her own fancy. It wasn't as if she didn't have Peggy's permission, after all. In fact, Peggy had almost begged her to make herself at home.

"With my luck," she'd said, "I'll be gone for two endless weeks on this abominable camping trip of Roger's and come home to find the contractor hasn't even shown up, much less installed my new whirlpool tub like he promised to do. And if that happens after I've spent an eternity in a tent in the woods light-years from civilization, I'll slit my wrists.''

"You can't," Cassie had told her, "because serious wrist-slitting requires a bathtub to sit in while you do it. And in any case, I couldn't allow you to eliminate one of Rent-a-Wife's best clients."

"Then you'll come and stay in my house and keep an eye on the contractor," Peggy announced. "If you're actually living right on the spot, he won't be able to make excuses."

Cassie hadn't been so sure; in her experience, workmen could be just as inventive on a daily basis as they could after the fact. But house-sitting was one of the services Rent-A-Wife had offered from the beginning, as was waiting for repairmen to show up so the person whose television or washing machine or furnace was misbehaving didn't have to take time off work. Peggy was really just asking for both services rolled into one—and flexibility in meeting the client's needs had been Rent-a-Wife's business credo from the very beginning. So Cassie was moving in for the duration.

Besides, she admitted, there were certain perks in having Peggy's townhouse all to herself—except, of course, for the workmen—for a couple of weeks. Terrace Square was neither the newest nor the most upscale development in the city, but it made Cassie's apartment complex look like the projects. Peggy's townhouse, with its high ceilings, sweeping curved staircase, and fancy glass, was a palace next to Cassie's efficiency apartment. And it wasn't just elegant, it was well built; Peggy could turn up her stereo system at any hour of the day or night without the worry of disturbing the neighbors. The idea of music at any hour and at any volume was, for Cassie, a sizeable inducement all by itself.

In fact, she decided, as soon as she got her things settled in the guest room she intended to try out Peggy's baby grand piano. Once the contractor started work, she'd no doubt have to keep the piano covered most of the time, to protect it from airborne dust, so she'd better enjoy it while she could.

She was hanging the last of her tailored pants outfits in the guest closet when the cell phone clipped to her belt cheeped. "Rent-a-Wife," she said absent-mindedly.

"It's eight in the evening, Cassie. You're not officially on duty any more," said one of her partners.

"Hi, Paige. It's habit, that's all."

"Are you getting settled in?"

"Oh, yes. Peggy may have to blast me out when she comes home. The thought of all this space—" Cassie caught at a jacket as it slipped off the hanger, and almost dropped the phone. "What were you saying, Paige?"

"I was asking if you could handle incoming calls tomorrow. Sabrina's going to Fort Collins to pick up a client's kid from a basketball training camp, and my mother has a doctor's appointment."

"Sure. I'll be right here, either waiting for the contractor to show up or standing over the crew while they work."

"Did Peggy really put that tight a restriction on you? Two weeks of it sounds a bit like a prison sentence."

"Oh, it won't be that bad. Once the work is started, I'll be able to keep an eye on the workers and still manage my regular schedule. When you forward the calls, Paige, would you use Peggy's number? My cell phone hasn't been holding a charge very well lately, and if I get swamped with calls..."

"We should be so lucky. It's the slow season, remember?"

And that, Cassie reminded herself, was an even better reason for taking on Peggy's project—because Peggy never quibbled about the bills, and this job would be a welcome bit of cash flow in a sluggish business period. "I know. If I was really smart I'd put up my Christmas tree now, because in a few months I'll be too busy dealing with customers' holiday needs to have time or energy for my own decorating."

"Precisely," Paige agreed. "And now that you mention holidays, maybe we should run a special. Maybe half-price on addressing Christmas cards if we can have them done before Halloween."

"Not a bad idea. But you'll have to wait till next year," Cassie warned, "so we can buy the cards *this* Christmas, when they're actually available. Is your mother all right?"

"It's just a checkup, but you know how long those can take. If everybody else is having an emergency, the routine patients wait. I'll switch the phone over to you first thing in the morning."

Cassie clipped her cell phone back on her belt, stashed her empty suitcases under the guest bed, and went downstairs to the big living room at the back of the townhouse.

Darkness had settled while she was upstairs, and the lower level of the house was dim, lit only by the glow of the antique-looking street lamps which lined the little playground park at the center of the townhouse complex. The bevelled glass panels beside the front door sliced and shattered the light, until nothing seemed to stay firmly in place in the silently shifting shadows. Even the stair balusters felt less than solid under her hand. Cassie shivered a little and hurried across the foyer.

Though the living room was open to the foyer, it had

a much warmer feel; thick pile carpet and deep, inviting upholstery formed a comforting contrast to the stark marble floors and hard edges of the foyer. The polished black surface of the baby grand gleamed even in the dimness, and Cassie ran a gentle hand over its glass-smooth beauty before she lifted the cover and tentatively touched a key.

Her fingers were stiff, but that was no surprise, for she hadn't played regularly in more than a year. Still, it felt surprisingly good to run a set of perfectly tuned scales, and it wasn't long before her hands seemed to have regained their command of the keys, finding their way almost instinctively to the next chord and the next and the next.

Cassie had never been a great pianist, for she'd managed only scattered lessons through the years, but she'd always enjoyed escaping into music. Though other instruments were too expensive to rent and too difficult to borrow, there was usually a piano to be found—at school, at church, in a friend's home, in the practice studios on campus—and so the piano had become her solace.

She played for a long while, softly wandering from one remembered favorite to another, stumbling now and then and having to work out a half-recalled passage. Only when she'd exhausted her repertoire did she look thoughtfully at the stack of music scores atop the cabinet next to the piano, wondering what treasures were buried there. Rent-a-Wife's unspoken ethical code meant that out of respect for a client, none of the partners would open any drawer or door unless she had been told to. But the music was right out in the open, and Peggy *had* told her to make herself at home....

Cassie found the sheet music for an old march and settled back at the piano to try out its first crashing chords. How satisfying it was, she thought, to play whatever she liked, knowing that the thick walls between the townhouse units would prevent the neighbors from being disturbed.

The march was a difficult one, and even with the help of a tiny spotlight atop the piano, the printed notes were faded and hard to read. Her first attempts at the opening chords were so dissonantly noisy that she didn't consciously hear the first heavy blow against the front door.

The second impact sounded like a battering ram striking home. In stunned shock, Cassie lifted her hands from the keyboard and—eyes widening in horror—stared across the foyer to the misshapen shadow which loomed outside the bevelled glass panels.

A burglar, she thought in frozen terror. Someone who thought the house was not only dark but empty. Someone, perhaps, who knew that the Abbotts had gone camping....

The third blow was the loudest of all—or perhaps it only seemed so because under its force the door frame splintered with an ear-piercing shriek. The door, torn halfway off its hinges, crashed against the foyer wall and rebounded, and suddenly the misshapen shadow resolved itself into the tallest, broadest-shouldered, and most threatening man Cassie had ever seen.

The glow of the small lamp which illuminated the sheet music felt suddenly like a floodlight, exposing her mercilessly. Instantly he focused on her—his eyes narrowing, his body tensing.

And then he spoke. His voice was deep, he sounded puzzled, and his question was the last thing she'd ever have expected a burglar to ask. "Just who the hell are you?"

The key wasn't where Roger always left it, under the silly pot of shaggy yellow flowers beside the front door of the townhouse.

What a surprise, Jake thought irritably. If his brother and sister-in-law insisted on using the most obvious hiding place ever invented, they ought to expect that someday an unauthorized person was likely to put their spare key to use.

Not only their friends and co-workers but the whole townhouse complex must have known they were leaving today to go camping for two weeks in Manitoba, unreachable unless somebody called in the Mounties; it was anybody's guess which of those people might have decided to take advantage of a couple of weeks' head start and lift a few valuables. They hadn't wasted any time, either— he guessed Roger and Peggy couldn't have been gone for more than six hours, and he'd bet their jewelry and silver flatware had almost followed them out the door.

Of course, it was simply Jake's bad luck that he'd be the one to find the key missing—and lord knew what other possessions as well.

Just what I wanted to do with the rest of my evening, he thought. Instead of the hot shower and much-overdue night's sleep he'd been looking forward to, he would no doubt have the pleasure of meeting a dozen or so Denver cops and seeing how they handled a burglary investigation.

Actually, he told himself, it would serve Roger and Peggy right if he just walked in and went straight to bed, ignoring until tomorrow morning whatever damage the burglar had done. Maybe, if the guy hadn't actually trashed the place, Jake could legitimately say that he'd been too tired to notice anything wrong, and so…

His hand was actually on the doorknob when he sighed and stopped himself. In good conscience, he couldn't put off reporting a crime. So he'd have to walk across the park in the center of the townhouse development to the office, tell whoever was in charge about the missing key, and suggest he or she call the police to check things out.

Besides, he realized abruptly, even if his principles would have let him sidestep the problem at least for the night, he couldn't just walk in—because the door was locked.

That seemed a bit odd; in his experience, burglars weren't likely to be sensitive about protecting people's remaining property after they'd helped themselves to whatever took their fancy. Perhaps this burglar was simply being cautious not to leave any obvious signs of his intrusion. And of course if he still had the key, he could come back anytime, if he was so inclined, to mop up the rest of the valuables....

Jake was turning away from the door when he heard an odd, dissonant crash from inside, and the locked door abruptly took on a whole new meaning. This was a very careful burglar indeed—one who was taking his time and wanted to be sure he wouldn't be interrupted. Though, if he didn't want to be noticed, why was he playing the stereo? Was he testing its sound quality to be sure it was worth his while to carry it away?

Adrenaline flooded through him, and without conscious decision Jake drew back, lowered his head, and in his best football-lineman style plunged his shoulder into the door.

It shuddered, but it held—which was more than he could say for the shoulder. Wincing, Jake took a step back and with all the power of his muscular legs thrust the sole of his shoe against the weakest spot on the door, right near the lock. Something cracked, and as he kicked once more the frame splintered and the door opened so abruptly that it banged against the far wall and rebounded, almost catching him square on the nose.

"So much for the element of surprise," he muttered

and stepped across the threshold, alert for movement, for strange shadows, for anything which was out of place.

What he saw in the faint glow of light from the living room took his breath away. The woman who faced him was young, white-faced, with a mop of curly red hair and the biggest eyes he'd ever seen. She had no flashlight, no mask, no dark clothes, no pry bar. She was wearing a tailored tweed jacket that would have fitted into any bank or board room in the city, and she was sitting bolt upright in front of Peggy's baby grand piano, her hands still arched above the keys.

All in all, she was the most unlikely-looking burglar he'd ever seen.

Which left him, Jake realized, with quite a problem.

Cassie had to swallow hard before she could find her voice. ''Who the hell am *I*? Who the hell are *you*? And I've got a lot better right to ask than you do, since I'm not the one making the unorthodox entry.'' She put her hands firmly on her hips, tentatively shifting her fingertips till she found the cell phone's keypad. Fortunately, she hadn't quite turned to face him, so even with the music light falling directly on her, he probably hadn't seen the phone still clipped to her belt. If, before he saw what she was doing, she could dial the emergency number by feel, then she could shout the address when a dispatcher answered....

She managed the first number, but instead of its usual cheerful cheep the phone made only a feeble groan, the last gasp of a dying battery. Cassie fumed and tried to remember where Peggy's nearest phone was located. Not that it mattered much, because whichever direction it was, the giant was between her and it.

And he was getting closer. While she'd been distracted,

he'd come halfway across the foyer. Close up he wasn't quite so tall or enormous as she'd thought at first; perhaps the wavering light behind him as he'd plunged through the doorway had magnified his physique. Still, he was plenty awe-inspiring.

"I'm waiting for an explanation," she reminded.

He reached for a panel of switches on the foyer wall and flipped them all. The living room's overhead lights glared, almost blinding her for a second, but as Cassie's eyes adjusted she got her first good look at him.

He was tall, all right—a bit over six feet, she guessed, with the shoulders to match his height—but part of the bulk she'd seen was actually the garment bag he was carrying slung from a strap over his shoulder.

That was hardly the sort of thing a burglar would choose to carry his tools, Cassie thought, and she felt her heartbeat slow a trifle.

"My name's Abbott," he said tersely. "And I'd like an explanation myself."

Cassie's eyes widened. She'd never met Roger Abbott, but judging from Peggy's occasional careless comments she'd never have expected him to be a cross between a major-league athlete and a dark-haired Greek god who lacked only an appropriate pedestal....

Whoa, she told herself. *This is your client's husband you're thinking about.*

Never judge an accountant by his job, she told herself. This one had probably worked his way through college as a bulldozer.

"I guess Peggy didn't tell you she'd hired a housesitter," she said. "But I thought you'd be halfway to Canada by now. What went wrong with the camping trip? And where's Peggy?"

"With Roger, I presume." He set the garment bag down and flexed his shoulder.

"Then you—" Cassie felt herself wavering. "What are you? A one-man SWAT team?"

He paused in mid-motion, eyes narrowing. "You sound like you were expecting one."

"Of course I wasn't. If you suppose you'll find anything illicit going on here, you've got the wrong house. The SWAT team is just the only faintly reasonable excuse I can think of to explain why you'd kick in the door."

"The key wasn't where it's supposed to be."

Cassie felt her jaw drop. Was the man on the lam from the loony bin? "*That's* why you broke in? You couldn't borrow an extra from the super? Though I suppose if you're not authorized to be here—"

"I'm authorized. I'm Roger's brother. I came to the door, I checked for the key, I heard noises inside what was supposed to be a very empty house—"

"Now I get it. You assumed *I* was the burglar, so you came plunging in to defend your brother's possessions."

"You don't think I'd kick in a stranger's door, do you?"

"Oh, I'm sure Roger and Peggy will find the fact very consoling, as they survey the damage, that at least you didn't damage a stranger's—"

He sighed. "Look, I'm tired and I'd really like to stop playing games, so let's cut to the bottom line. You're right about one thing—Peggy *didn't* tell me she'd hired a house-sitter. Of course that might be because I didn't talk to her, but Roger didn't mention you either. I suppose you have some credentials to prove you're actually who you say you are?"

"Upstairs in my handbag. And I'm sure you won't mind showing me your driver's license."

He scowled a little.

"Fair's fair," Cassie pointed out. "Anybody could pretend to be Roger Abbott's brother."

"I can't imagine why anyone would want to." He tugged a slim leather wallet from his hip pocket.

"Great family feeling you have, don't you?" Cassie jibed. "Now I remember hearing about you—Peggy told me you didn't even come to their wedding last year."

"She makes a great story out of it."

"Well, he *is* your brother—"

"And it was his third wedding. With all the practice I've had at being an usher at Roger's weddings, I could have phoned in my performance. Besides, I was just starting a new job in Florida at the time, but Peggy never seems to remember that bit. Are you interested in my ID, or not?"

Cassie reached for the laminated card he'd extracted from his wallet and studied it with deliberation. His name was Jake Abbott, she noted. Hadn't she wrapped a gift for a Jake, in that day-long spree last Christmas? She was sure of it—and just as certain that it had been something completely outrageous. Tickets for a real-life dogfight in a military jet, perhaps?

According to his driver's license, he lived in Manhattan, somewhere on the lower end of the island if she recalled the street system correctly.

Obviously the job in Florida hadn't lasted long, she thought. She wondered if he was only making a visit to Denver or if the Manhattan address was obsolete as well.

But of course the other information was still current. He was six feet exactly and weighed one-eighty, and his eyes were brown. And the picture on the license—though hardly magazine-cover quality—was distinctly of the same man who was watching her with thinly disguised impatience.

She handed the license back. "Okay, I'm convinced you're who you say you are, Mr. Abbott."

"Good. Now it's my turn. Who are you?"

"Cassie Kerrigan," she said, "I'm a partner in Rent-a-Wife, and Peggy hired me to—"

"Rent a *what?*" He paused, wallet half into his pocket. "And you say *Peggy* hired you?"

Cassie wanted to groan. "All right, don't let your imagination roam. Rent-a-Wife is not an escort service—"

"I was thinking more in terms of a bordello that delivers. Sort of like phoning out for pizza."

"That," Cassie snapped, "was obvious. Rent-a-Wife is in the business of providing personal service, something like a concierge does in a big hotel. We take care of the sort of time-consuming details that clutter up a working person's schedule, making life smoother and easier. But we don't dust, we don't wash windows, we don't watch babies, and we certainly don't indulge in kinky—" she paused. "Why am I explaining this to you?"

"Perhaps it's because you feel defensive about your profession," he said smoothly.

"Only about the name," she admitted. "If we'd given it a little more thought, we'd have called it Helping Hands or something instead. If you'll wait here, I'll go get the proof you asked for."

Jake shook his head. "Don't bother."

"Why not? You aren't suddenly going to tell me that my honest face has convinced you I'm telling the truth?"

"No, though the no-kinky-sex line came close. If you were in that business, you'd call it Rent-a-Lover."

"Thanks for the input. I'll be sure to pass your comments along at our next board meeting."

"My pleasure." He rubbed his shoulder again. "Roger must have forgotten about you when he told me I could borrow the house for a while, because he didn't say a word about me having company."

"Well, nobody warned me either. Maybe Peggy didn't tell him I'd be here. Communication seems to be their weak point, doesn't it? Peggy hires me, Roger loans the house to you—"

"You think maybe he didn't tell her I needed a place to stay for a few weeks?"

Well, Cassie mused, *I didn't really think that he was just dropping by—all the way from Manhattan—to pick up his brother's mail.* "I think maybe he had a good reason for not telling her you were coming to town," she said crisply. "Is this another new job? Or are you simply between periods of employment at the moment?"

"Oh, it's a new job. And now that you mention it, I can picture Roger forgetting to bring it up with Peggy."

Cassie said, with the barest tinge of sarcasm, "He was probably too busy getting ready for the camping trip to think about details like an unexpected house guest."

Jake shrugged. "I can't see that it much matters how the misunderstanding happened. The point is, there's no need for you to stay. Since I'm going to be here for a while, a house-sitter would only be in my way."

"On the other hand," Cassie murmured, "maybe Roger *did* tell Peggy you were coming, and she thought it would be a good idea to have someone on hand to counter your violent tendencies." She shot a glance at the door, still half-open and hanging by one hinge. "Too bad she didn't warn me that you haven't learned how to ring a doorbell, but—"

"What's the matter, Ms. Kerrigan? Upset at losing your cushy job before you'd even got a good start on it?"

"You didn't hire me," Cassie pointed out. "And you can't fire me."

"If you insist on staying, you can't prevent me from speculating about why you're so anxious to stick around." His voice had gone suddenly silky.

"Like I'm seizing an excuse to get to know you better?" Cassie shuddered artistically. "I ought to take you at your word. I'm sure you'll positively enjoy dealing with the workmen."

She brushed past him and started toward the stairway.

"What workmen?" The suggestive note was gone from Jake's voice.

She didn't look back. "The ones who are going to start tearing out walls tomorrow."

"Walls?"

"You don't think Peggy was so nervous about leaving home that she wanted someone to guard her lipstick and her collection of ruffly pillows, do you? If it wasn't for the workmen, she wouldn't *need* a house-sitter. But I suppose since you're here now, I could just tell her that you insisted on taking over—"

"I don't have time for stuff like that."

"Of course not," Cassie soothed. "Your new job—whatever it is—must be far too important to leave you time to supervise workmen. So why don't you go check into a hotel and let me carry on here?"

"Because I don't like hotels."

Cassie pursed her lips thoughtfully. "I suppose what you really mean is that you don't want to give up the free rent. Not that I blame you—until you know if this job is going to last, obviously you don't want to run up any extra bills."

"Who put the bee in your bonnet?" He sounded

amused. "I'm not expecting to get fired, if that makes you feel better."

Cassie bit her tongue. Just because the man had accidently trod on a couple of her hot buttons didn't make his job or his way of life any of her business. "What a relief that must be for you," she said gently, "considering that of course you're going to have to pay to fix the door. Luckily the contractor is going to be here anyway, so you can—"

"Don't try to dodge your share of the blame."

"*My* share? I had nothing to do with your faulty decision-making! I was just sitting here minding my own business, enjoying my music—"

"Which sounded like a roomful of tortured cats. If it hadn't been for that raucous noise, I would have gone across to the super's office and gotten a key."

"So instead you burst in to rescue the suffering felines? Thank you," Cassie said politely. "I'm so glad you liked my performance. Now if you'll knock off the distractions and get back to the subject.... Come to think of it, I'm glad you're not going to a hotel. You're not going to dump this mess on me—a front door that won't even close, much less lock, and..."

"And which is practically an invitation to ravishers," Jake added. "So why don't *you* go home? At least, I assume you have a home, unless Peggy found you living in a cardboard box under a bridge somewhere."

"Because of the workmen. I told you."

"Surely you could check on them now and then without actually living here."

"Peggy wanted me to be here every morning to let them in—as sort of a check system to be sure the job's progressing on schedule. To get all the way across town to do that, I'd have to leave my cardboard box under the bridge at a mighty uncomfortable hour. That's why Peggy suggested I stay here instead." She waved a careless hand toward the entrance. "Not that letting the workers in tomorrow will take any extra effort, with the shape the front door's in."

"You're not going to give up, are you?"

"*I* was hired to do a job. *You* were offered a favor. There's no comparison between our reasons for being here, so if one of us leaves, it isn't going to be me. If you insist on hanging around, I'll just consider you an additional obstacle."

"Fine." Jake yawned. "Suit yourself. As for me, I'm tired, it's late, I've had a long flight and I have work to do before my first meeting tomorrow. So I'm going to bed."

"What about the door?"

"I'll prop a chair under it."

"Oh, that makes me feel *very* safe."

"And you suggested I go off to a hotel and leave you here alone and unprotected," Jake chided. "How could I possibly be so crass?"

Cassie sighed. She'd never heard such an unconvincing tone of voice in her life.

"But I draw the line at dragging a couch in from the living room and spending the night blocking the door with my body, in order to protect you from the bogeymen."

"I wouldn't dream of letting you give up your beauty sleep for my sake, when you're obviously set on impressing your new boss tomorrow."

"And you're obviously capable of taking care of yourself."

"Don't you doubt it for a minute," Cassie recommended.

Jake grinned lazily, and Cassie felt the impact all the

way to her toes. "If you think that I'm likely to forget myself and wander into your bedroom," he murmured, "don't stay awake hoping." He patted back another yawn. "I suppose—considering the cardboard box under the bridge and all—that you've already claimed the master suite, but I'll tell you what. I'll flip you for it."

Cassie let her gaze drop modestly, so he wouldn't see the amusement she couldn't quite smother. Why ruin the surprise by telling him now that as of tomorrow morning the master bath was going to be history? "Actually, I'm in the guest bedroom. A certain delicacy made me think better of moving into my employer's own private quarters, so—"

Jake rolled his eyes. "Delicacy? Well, a little thing like that isn't going to keep *me* from getting a good night's sleep."

Cassie said sweetly, "I never imagined that it would."

CHAPTER TWO

ALL things considered, Cassie slept surprisingly well. The guest room was comfortable, and there wasn't a strange sound, either from the master suite or the foyer downstairs, to disturb her rest.

But the first gleam of sunlight through the guest room window brought her fully awake. She was almost looking forward to her next skirmish with Jake Abbott, especially because she'd be going into this one backed up by a bunch of burly workmen armed with wrecking bars.

Peggy's contractor was as good as his word. When the doorbell rang promptly at seven, Cassie looked approvingly at her watch and cautiously dragged the straight chair out from under the knob where Jake had propped it last night, hoping the door wouldn't crumble as she opened it.

The young man standing on the step smoothly moved his toothpick from one corner of his mouth to the other without using his hands. "Morning, Miz Abbott," he said in a voice as slow-moving as cold taffy. "I'm Buddy Nelson, here to start work on your hot tub."

He was younger than Cassie had expected, certainly not over thirty, and he wasn't exactly the burly bruiser she'd been picturing—lanky would have been a better description. He was wearing stained, crumpled jeans that would have been rejected by any self-respecting rag bag, and his faded flannel shirt sported a triangular tear right in front, displaying a good portion of hairy chest. He hadn't shaved

23

in the better part of a week, Cassie guessed, and a rubber band held his hair back in a tight, greasy ponytail.

And he was alone. Where was the crew she'd expected?

"I'm not Mrs. Abbott," Cassie said. "I'm—"

Buddy was staring past her at the door. "Had a little trouble here, I see," he said with a nasal twang.

"You might say so. As long as you're going to be working here anyway, Mr. Abbott will want to talk to you about the best way to fix it."

He looked at her a little oddly. "*Fix* it, ma'am?"

Cassie had no trouble seeing what he meant. In daylight, she noted, the damage looked worse than when it had been fresh last night. The door wasn't even wood, she realized; instead, it was made of some kind of fibrous white stuff with a wood-grained film laid over the top and painted teal-blue, and instead of splintering like wood it had torn into twisted, irregular fragments. She suspected there was no way it could ever be glued back together.

"I mean fix the problem, not necessarily this particular door." Why was she even discussing the matter, anyway? The door wasn't her responsibility. She stepped back into the foyer. "If you'll come in, Mr. Nelson, I'll ask Mr. Abbott to come down right now, so you can talk about the door before your crew gets here."

"No crew," he drawled. "There's just me."

Cassie opened her mouth to ask how he planned to manhandle a whirlpool tub big enough for two bathers entirely by himself, and then she shut it again. Surely Peggy wouldn't have hired the man if she'd had any doubts of his abilities. Would she?

On the other hand, Cassie thought, if Peggy had ever seen him in person, he wouldn't have mistaken Cassie for the Mrs. Abbott who had hired him.

The contractor's slow, twangy voice went steadily on.

"I like to take my time and get things just right. And by the way, call me Buddy. Mr. Nelson always makes me think of my dad. I wouldn't hardly know how to answer to that."

Cassie thought, *And that would make two of us who were struck speechless.*

She was halfway up the stairs by the time Buddy had stepped across the threshold, and when she glanced back, he was carefully rocking the door on its one remaining hinge. Was he simply fascinated by the damage, she wondered, or did he always move that slowly? Either way, it didn't bode well for the chances of Peggy's project being finished on time.

Cassie was beginning to get a squeamish feeling in the pit of her stomach. *This could be a very long couple of weeks*, she told herself.

Cassie hadn't heard a sound from the master bedroom since she'd wakened, and she'd been particularly cautious herself about making noise as she showered and dressed. The man had said he was tired, so she was letting him sleep in, she'd told herself sanctimoniously. It wasn't her fault if Jake Abbott got a rude awakening now.

She rapped loudly, and was disappointed when without even a second's hesitation Jake said, "Come in."

Cassie pushed the door open a few inches. "You see? *That's* how it's done—you tap your knuckles against the wood, and the other person responds with an invitation to enter."

She was even more disappointed to see that he was already dressed for the business day. The jacket which matched his charcoal trousers was still draped across the bed, but his white shirt was immaculate, and his dark-red tie was already in place. Cassie had no trouble putting a value on his tailoring; she'd ferried enough silk ties, monogrammed shirts, and custom-made suits to and from dry cleaners in the last year to know precisely what she was looking at. He was obviously intending to make an impression on his new boss. "You're a morning person, I see."

"Not really, but my body thinks it's still in another time zone. I've been up for two hours." He was sitting at a fragile decorative table near the window with a palm-top computer open in front of him, and he barely looked up. "To what do I owe this interruption?"

"Well, it's not because I have an overwhelming desire to see whether you wear pajamas," Cassie said tartly. "The contractor's here."

"I'll talk to him later."

"Not much later, I'm afraid," she said, trying hard to keep the note of glee out of her voice, "because the first place he's going to start work is in there." She pointed at the door to the master bath.

Jake turned to face her. "Tearing out walls, you said."

Cassie smothered a grin at the hollow note in his voice. "I'm afraid I may have forgotten to give you the details last night."

"You know perfectly well you didn't tell me. No wonder you were so gracious about letting me have this room."

"It must have been the sheer joy of exchanging views with you that made the need to warn you slip my mind. But you might take a minute to cover up anything you don't want to get extremely dusty."

The way he started muttering under his breath cautioned Cassie not to wait for a clearer answer, but she'd barely gotten to the door before he called, "I really don't need to talk to the contractor. Just tell him to replace the door and send me a bill."

"Oh, no," Cassie said airily. "I couldn't possibly give him that message, because it would rob you of the pleasure of meeting Buddy."

She had just set foot on the marble floor of the foyer when she heard Jake, still muttering, at the top of the stairs. Pleased with the reaction she'd provoked, Cassie smiled sweetly at the contractor and strolled on through the hallway toward the kitchen.

She was checking Peggy's pantry for basic supplies when the phone rang. Paige had been as good as her word about switching over the calls first thing, Cassie thought; it was barely seven-thirty in the morning.

It wasn't a client on the other end of the line, however, but Rent-a-Wife's third partner.

"Sabrina?" Cassie said in surprise. "I thought you were on your way to Fort Collins." She balanced the phone on her shoulder, leaving both hands free to shift boxes and cans out of her way so she could see what was behind them.

"I will be soon, and I probably won't be back till late. Why aren't you answering your cell phone?"

"I turned it off when I plugged it in to recharge. The battery needs all the breaks it can get because I'll probably have to use it later today when I run out for groceries. How'd you know where to find me?"

"Paige, of course—I caught her just as she was going out the door to take Eileen to the doctor. You'll be at our lunch meeting tomorrow, won't you?"

Cassie sighed. "I'd almost forgotten what day it was. Sure, I'll be there."

"Can you come a little early? There's something I'd like to talk to you about."

"Without Paige?" Cassie frowned. "Is Eileen all right?

Paige told me it was a routine checkup, but she seemed to be expecting it to take most of the day."

"Nothing's really routine when you're confined to a wheelchair," Sabrina pointed out. "But it's not Eileen that's bothering me, it's a client. I just want your opinion of something."

"Of course," Cassie said slowly. "Will half an hour be enough?"

The hair on the back of her neck suddenly rose to attention, but before she could react a voice behind her said, "Is that call for me?"

Cassie's hand jerked, and an economy-sized bag of flour, already teetering on the edge of the shelf, tipped off and smacked against the floor. The paper wrapper split in a dozen places and a small white cloud rose silently from the wreckage.

"Is that your workman?" Sabrina asked. "I knew I was going to envy you this job—he sounds like the brawny, muscular, forceful type."

Cassie looked over her shoulder to see Jake standing in the kitchen doorway. He'd put on his jacket, though it was casually drawn back so he could thrust one hand in his trouser pocket, and he was carrying a slim briefcase. Last night, with tired eyes and a five-o'clock shadow, he'd been a very good-looking man. This morning, rested and groomed, he was not far from perfection.

Appearances can be deceiving, Cassie reminded herself.

"Try aggressive, domineering, and testosterone-ridden," she suggested.

"It's all in your perspective, darling," Sabrina murmured. "And to think while you're watching muscles ripple, I'm going to be stuck in a car with an adolescent male who's still in braces. I can't wait to hear all about the man who goes with that luscious voice. Over lunch tomorrow?''

Cassie wanted to swear, but she knew that would only increase Sabrina's curiosity. "Maybe we should meet an hour early," she said sweetly.

"No, dear. I won't let you start till Paige gets there, because it'll save me the trouble of repeating it all if she gets the details first-hand, too.''

Cassie bit her tongue and put the phone down.

Jake set his briefcase on the counter and moved out of the doorway. Cassie watched as, almost absently, he rubbed the point of his shoulder. "Who was on the phone?''

"A friend of mine," she said gently. "If that call had been for you, believe me, I'd have let you know. You don't have to sneak around and eavesdrop.''

"I wasn't trying to. I thought you heard me, anyway, because you started to vibrate the moment I walked in.''

Cassie bristled at the suggestion, and then told herself not to be silly. If Jake didn't already know that her automatic reaction to his presence had been the direct opposite of sensual, there was no point in trying to explain it.

In fact, he didn't sound interested at all. "You're not exactly a firecracker yourself," he said. "I've never known a woman who could be so quiet in the morning.''

"Have a lot of experience?" Cassie asked idly, and caught herself just an instant too late. "No, wait—I withdraw the question, because I don't want to leave the impression that I could possibly be interested in the answer.'' She reached into the bottom of the pantry closet for a dustpan and began to scoop up the spilled flour. "How did you and Buddy get along?''

"Fairly well, I think. Of course, the first thing I had to do was get his attention off you."

She straightened abruptly, almost dropping the dustpan. "Off *me*? What do you mean? The only thing he had eyes for was the mess you'd made of the door."

"Not by the time I got there. What did you do, cast a spell over the man? Though even I, as a neutral observer, have to admit that the show you put on as you walked down the hall was worth watching."

"What are you talking about?"

"You can't expect me to believe you weren't swaying your hips on purpose, Ms. Kerrigan."

"Sometimes people see what they expect to see," Cassie snapped. He grinned, and she reminded herself that there was no point wasting time trying to convince him, when he'd obviously reached the only conclusion he was capable of. "But we'd already established that you have a mind which runs along those tracks. What about the door?"

"Buddy says he's not in the door-replacement business."

Cassie blinked. "What? He's a contractor."

"A *plumbing* contractor. He does sinks and tubs and dishwashers and water heaters. Not doors. He explained it all to me very patiently."

From the faintly ironic twist in Jake's voice, Cassie had no trouble imagining Buddy's recitation of the excruciating details about his job. "So now what?"

"I'll talk to the superintendent."

She shook her head. "It won't do you any good. The homeowners' association fee here at Terrace Square covers outside maintenance only."

Jake shrugged. "Half the door's on the outside. Does that count?"

"I mean stuff like grass-cutting and snow removal. Things which apply only to one unit are the responsibility of the individual owner. Or, in this case, the responsibility of the person who—"

Jake fiddled with the clasps on his briefcase. He wasn't looking at Cassie, which made warning bells go off in the back of her brain. "Maybe you could talk to Buddy," he suggested. "Persuade him to change his mind."

"Wiggle my hips a little, you mean? Forget it. In the first place, you're hallucinating if you think that could change Buddy's mind. And in the second place, it's not my problem. Remember, Jake? I'm not the one who broke the door down. *You* are."

"Okay."

Cassie eyed him warily. Even the little experience she'd had with Jake Abbott didn't lead her to believe that he'd give up on anything so easily.

"In the meantime," he said cheerfully, "I guess I owe you an apology."

"Oh, this ought to be good," Cassie muttered.

"For trying to talk you into leaving last night, I mean. It turns out to be a good thing after all that Peggy hired a house-sitter, because as long as you're here, keeping an eye on the situation—"

"No, you don't," Cassie said hastily. "I was hired to watch the contractor. I never said I'd sit by the front door for days on end like a security guard. If you think I'm going to babysit this house till you get around to finding someone to install a new door..."

Jake's eyes were bright, expectant. "It seems to be a somewhat unusual door, too," he mused. "I don't suppose you noticed that it doesn't match the ones in the rest of the townhouses. I'd never paid attention, but of course

Buddy saw that right away. He seemed to think it could be quite a project even to find a match.''

"But then, what does Buddy know about it? If he said himself that he doesn't do doors..."

"He knows contractors, though. And he said at this season, in this climate, they've all got their hands full with jobs they've promised to finish before winter sets in.''

Cassie capitulated. "All right,'' she said hollowly. "I'll talk to Buddy. But I'm not promising anything.''

"Do you mean you're not promising results to me, or incentives to Buddy?''

Cassie clenched her fists. "If you mean what I think you mean by *incentives*—''

Jake's eyebrows climbed. "What a picturesque mind you have, Ms. Kerrigan. For all you know, I was suggesting you bake his favorite cake. As a matter of fact, you've got enough flour on you that it looks as if you've already started.'' He rubbed his shoulder again. "And as long as we're speaking of food, is there anything to eat around here? In all the confusion I think I forgot dinner last night.''

"Didn't they feed you on the plane?''

"That stuff isn't food. It's made of experimental plastics.''

"There's a package of burritos in the freezer, I think.''

"I couldn't face a frozen burrito at this hour of the morning.''

"Remember?'' Cassie chided. "This isn't a hotel. Or even a bed and breakfast.''

"And I suppose Peggy cleaned out the refrigerator.''

"Before leaving for two weeks? I should hope so; wouldn't you have?'' Then she remembered a job she'd done a while back, for an elderly bachelor in a high-rise apartment. After scraping the mold out of his refrigerator,

Cassie had not only thrown away the rubber gloves she'd used, but she hadn't been able to eat anything green for a month. "Don't answer that."

"I don't mind. I don't have to clean it out, because—"

"I'm already sorry I asked," Cassie pointed out. "I suppose, with the way you move around, you just leave the mess behind for the landlord to deal with."

"Not quite. If all you keep in a refrigerator is ketchup, olives, and a few cans of beer, you never have to clean it out because there's nothing to spoil."

"And you're complaining because all Peggy left you is a frozen burrito? I'm surprised you don't consider it a gourmet meal. And I'm disappointed, too. Don't you even keep white wine on hand for the ladies in your life?"

"Nope. I take them out so they can drink whatever they want." He opened the refrigerator door and studied the nearly bare shelves. "I think you're right about the communications problem between Roger and Peggy. If he'd known the details about this little remodeling project, he'd have warned me. And if Peggy had known I was coming—"

"She'd have left your favorite brands in the refrigerator, I suppose." Cassie dumped the broken flour bag in the garbage can. "I'll be going grocery shopping sometime today. Is there anything you'd like?"

He stopped staring at the refrigerator shelves and turned to inspect her. Suspicion sharpened his features till he looked as if he'd been chiseled in stone. "You mean you'd actually do that?"

Annoyed, Cassie snapped, "I'd be delighted to pick up whatever you need—besides the ingredients for Buddy's cake, of course, which you can expect to pay for. You see, Rent-a-Wife not only charges a flat fee per hour for our services, but on shopping jobs we add a percentage of the final bill. I could use a little extra spending money right now, so if there's anything at all you'd like…''

"I should have known there'd be a catch. Yeah, get me some ketchup and olives and—"

Cassie sighed. "Green or black?"

"Both."

"And what brand of beer?"

The phone rang shrilly, and automatically Cassie reached across the counter to answer it. "Rent-a-Wife. This is Cassie."

There was a long silence at the other end of the line, and only when Cassie repeated herself did she get an answer. A low, rich, masculine voice said, "I must have made a mistake. I'm trying to reach Jake Abbott, and I swear he told me he'd be at this number."

Cassie winced. "He's right here. Just a moment."

There was a sudden snort of laughter from the man on the line. "Rent a *wife*, did you say? And he just got into town last night—what a fast mover!"

Cassie ignored him and held out the phone. Jake took it, but when she would have slipped past him and down the hall, he stepped firmly in front of her, blocking her into the kitchen.

"Good morning," he said, and a moment later, "Of course, Caleb. Eleven o'clock is fine." His gaze focused on Cassie. "No, you heard correctly. That's what she said."

When he put the phone down, it was with a calm deliberation that Cassie found far more frightening than a slam. "That call was about my business meeting."

"I gathered that." She shrugged. "Don't feel you owe me any explanations."

"I'm not explaining, I'm making a point. That was

Caleb Tanner, one of the most powerful men in Colorado..."

"Is he your new boss? How nice for you. Of course, it's just my luck—I could have scraped an acquaintance with the famous Caleb Tanner, but I missed my chance. It's funny such an important guy makes his own phone calls, though, don't you think?"

"If I may have your attention, Ms. Kerrigan.... Occasionally the people I'm working with will be calling me. You've already given him a very wrong impression—"

"No," Cassie corrected. "He may have jumped to a very wrong conclusion, based on no evidence, but that's not my fault."

"If you'd shown a speck of forethought when you named your business, I'd be more sympathetic. Would you like to hear his opinion of Rent-a-Wife?"

"I don't think so."

"He said it sounded to him like an idea whose time had come. The last thing I want is a repetition—so don't answer the phone again."

Cassie thoughtfully rubbed a fingertip against the bridge of her nose. "Are you finished?" she asked pleasantly.

"I think I've made myself clear."

"So now it's my turn to make my point, right? If I may have your attention, Mr. Abbott.... I was here first, I have dibs on the phone and I'm not working for a business, I'm running one, right from this kitchen. So you have three choices. Hire me to find you an apartment, tell Mr. Important Tanner that you've got a party line—" She sidestepped him and turned on her heel in the doorway. "Or just spend all your time in his office so he won't need to call. Which would not only be better for your job performance, but—from my point of view—would be a gift from heaven!''

Tanner Electronics was not unlike many of the businesses Jake visited in the course of a year's work. It was a young firm trying to disguise itself as well-established, and the tell-tale signs were all there: carpet so new it still smelled of factory chemicals, expensive office furniture cheek-by-jowl with pieces that looked as if they'd come from the Salvation Army's dumpster, staff who looked more like they'd been tearing out walls with Buddy the contractor rather than designing delicate electronics.

Yet, even in the midst of confusion there was an air of excitement about the place that few older businesses could maintain. The workers might look like a ragtag bunch, but Jake's experience told him it wasn't out of disrespect for a dress code; they were just too busy thinking up new gadgets to worry about whether their jeans were clean.

The wild contrasts Jake had noted as soon as he stepped inside the front door followed him all the way to the corner office of the chief executive. Outside Caleb Tanner's office was a richly carpeted room with a half-dozen good art prints on the walls but not a stick of furniture, much less a secretary. *No wonder he makes his own calls*, Jake thought.

The door to the inner office stood open, and Jake approached it, intending to announce himself. As he stepped through the doorway, however, a feminine giggle tickled his ears. ''Here, darling,'' the woman said breathlessly. ''Let me help you take it off.''

It was too late to tactfully back out; the man sitting on the corner of the desk, arms crossed and both hands clutching the ribbed bottom of a brilliantly colored ski sweater, had already seen him. ''Are you Abbott?''

Jake nodded. "Sorry," he said. "But the door was open." He held out a hand, noting from the corner of his eye the displeasure displayed by the statuesque blonde standing so close to Caleb Tanner that there was scarcely room for a sheet of paper between them. Only then did he realize that the ski sweater Caleb Tanner was wearing had just one sleeve.

Caleb tugged the sweater over his head with one swift, graceful move and handed it to the blonde. "Sorry, Angelique," he said. "Business calls me." He slid off the desk and returned Jake's handshake.

The blonde pouted elegantly. "Oh, all right. I'll see you tonight, darling, but I don't know how I'll be able to wait." She blew Caleb a kiss, folded the sweater over her arm, and paused to give Jake the once-over. Her displeasure seemed to have vanished, for she gave him a slow blink and slower smile. Caleb didn't seem to notice; he was watching Jake as the blonde went out into the hall with a suggestive wiggle.

Overdone, Jake thought, remembering Cassie Kerrigan's much more subtle style. And the blonde was all hair and no substance, too. Not at all like Cassie, who had plenty of substance along with a mop of hair so unruly a man could play with it for a year and not—

Cassie Kerrigan's hair is not the issue at the moment, he reminded himself, and looked curiously around Caleb Tanner's office.

Here, too, contradictions abounded. The desk on which Caleb had been sitting was teak, a massively elegant piece which should be topped with nothing more than a blotter and a pen stand. Instead, it had apparently been turned into a workbench; circuits, tools and bits of electronic gear lay everywhere, and the fine surface was gouged along the edge and marred by deep scratches.

Caleb shrugged into a corduroy jacket and gestured toward a couple of chairs in the corner of the office. "Sorry to give the impression I was doing a strip tease. Angelique's making the sweater, so she insisted I try it to be sure the sleeves were the right length."

Jake had his doubts. He remembered the rhythmic click of his grandmother's knitting needles and the concentration required to follow her patterns. Caleb's blonde didn't seem the type. But it was hardly polite on a first face-to-face meeting—and a business one at that—to say any such thing. "A talented young woman," he said levelly.

Caleb's gaze turned shrewd. "Which means you don't think she can count high enough to keep track of the stitches. I've had some questions along those lines myself—along with wondering whether she's really knitting me a sweater or plotting to construct a strait jacket." He leaned back in his chair. "You know, Jake, I think you're onto something with this rent-a-wife business."

"As far as that goes…" Jake began.

"It makes a whole lot of sense. If you just rent a wife when you need one, you avoid all the mess of getting rid of her when you don't." He leaned back in his chair. "But I'm sure that isn't what you came to talk about. What do you think of my little recording device?"

"I've been playing with it," Jake said. "Along with every other product you've been manufacturing. It's no wonder you've swept the market with the audiophiles, that's sure—you're giving them incredible quality for the money. I just wish I was as sure of the future of the next gadget."

Caleb's eyebrows raised. "You don't think all those people who have video-cassette recorders which constantly blink midnight because they're too hard to program won't jump on a technology that lets them simply talk to their television sets?''

''There are similar things out there.''

''Oh, no. With all the others you have to look up the time and the channel and plug in the numbers. With my little toy, all you have to do is tell the machine to record all the episodes of whatever series you want, and it'll find them no matter where or when. Plus once it's recorded a program, it won't bother with the reruns, and it'll automatically play them back in sequence if you want. Throw in digital quality recording, with no videotape to degrade or break—''

''In other words, your gadget improves everything about television-watching except the program content.''

Caleb grinned. ''I guess you have a point there. Of course, you *could* use it to keep up with educational TV, but—''

''That's part of the problem. You're going to be very high-end on this product. I don't see any way around it, and I wonder how many people are excited enough about sit-com reruns to invest the kind of money you're going to be asking for the machine.''

''The market research shows—''

Jake said, coolly, ''Market research will show anything it's set up to show.'' He watched Caleb Tanner closely, half-expecting an explosion. But the only reaction was a muscle twitching in the man's jaw. ''Perhaps,'' Jake went on, ''if you'd adapt the basic idea to existing equipment by making the automatic recording feature simply an add-on to regular videotape machines—''

''License it, you mean. If I let those manufacturers get their hands on the prototype, they'd copy it in a New York minute.''

Jake shook his head. ''They'd have the same marketing

difficulties you will, if they tried to manufacture a stand-alone product. If you piggyback it to existing technology, you wouldn't be asking people to make such an enormous shift.''

''And I wouldn't be giving them much in return for their money, either. I'd be dumbing down a great idea. The change you're suggesting would mean giving up the digital storage capability and sacrificing things like instantaneous search and playback features.''

''It would also mean selling three times as many units at half the price.''

Caleb considered and shook his head. ''Not worth the sacrifice. I wouldn't want to put my name on it.''

''I'm not sure enough of those people whose videotape units are collecting dust will pay the price for yet another new technology.''

''Even if it leapfrogs everything else out there?''

''Because something is better than the competing products doesn't mean it's automatically going to be successful. At least not without a major marketing push, and that will be very expensive.''

Caleb shrugged. ''Stock offerings and venture capital and all that stuff has never been quite in my line, you know. That's where you come in, Jake. It's your job to find the money to do it all.''

Not quite, Jake wanted to say.

But Caleb had jumped up. ''So you'll need to see everything, won't you? Let me take you out to the factory and show you what Tanner Electronics can do.''

''That was next on my list,'' Jake said.

Caleb frowned, and Jake felt a sudden frisson of excitement. What had Caleb Tanner suddenly recalled? What didn't he want Jake to see?

"I hope you don't mind if we take my motorcycle," Caleb confided. "I've got an extra helmet, of course."

Jake tried to smother a smile. He'd been warned Caleb Tanner was an original—but it appeared that might turn out to be an understatement.

CHAPTER THREE

THOUGH the day had been pleasant, by evening the wind had risen, and every time the townhouse creaked Cassie half expected the cobbled-together front door to collapse in a heap. But simply watching it wasn't going to keep it in place, she told herself. Deliberately, she made herself stop pacing and retreated to the kitchen to microwave a frozen dinner.

She was simply suffering from a good case of nerves, she told herself. Anyone would, in the circumstances. The fact that she had neither seen nor heard from Jake since he'd walked out of the kitchen that morning had nothing to do with it.

Nothing at all.

Maybe he'd gone to a hotel after all, she decided as she picked at her turkey tetrazzini. It just didn't seem like him, though, to make the move without at least telling her.

In fact, she doubted that he'd have simply announced his plans. No matter what his actual excuse, Jake Abbott would have put forth a logical reason why leaving was his own decision, completely to his benefit, and not in any way because Cassie had suggested it!

She put the remainder of her dinner in the trash compactor and settled in the living room with a coffee table full of projects, enough to keep her too busy all evening to think about the door. And as for Jake…if it wasn't for his perfidy in leaving her stuck with the mess he'd created, she'd be celebrating the fact that he wasn't anywhere to be found.

But her heart wasn't in writing personal notes to prospective Rent-a-Wife clients, and when she realized she'd started addressing a packet to "Dear Jake," Cassie crumpled the pamphlet into a ball, tossed her pen down in frustration, and turned her attention to her cell phone.

She was trying to wrestle the lid off the battery compartment when there was a loud knock at the front door. She stared at it for a moment, then scrambled to her feet, stiff from sitting with her legs folded under her, and went to peek out through the beveled glass.

And the only reason her heart leaped at the sight of Jake, she told herself sternly, was that—much as she hated to admit it—she *had* been just a little scared to be there by herself. She'd have been just as happy to see the superintendent, or the woman next door, or Buddy....

Well, maybe not Buddy, she amended as she pulled the door open.

"You're a fast learner," she said admiringly. "It took only one lesson in how to knock, and you've got it down cold!"

"I thought it might be safer this way. Besides, I still don't have a key." Gingerly, he took hold of the knob and moved the door slowly back and forth. "Hey, this isn't half bad. How'd you manage to get it back in working order?"

"Buddy tightened it up a little."

His smile was like a summer sunrise. "I knew you could persuade him."

"Well, it's a long way from fixed. You can actually hear the wind howling through the cracks."

"Maybe we can get a sound-effects company to come

in and record the noise for their next haunted-house package.''

''And if you think the noise is bad, wait till you feel the draft. Be careful closing it, all right? Buddy wanted to board it up entirely because he said it would be safer not to use it at all.''

''And you don't think he'd be pleased if he came back tomorrow and had to do it all over again.''

''Next time, you get to convince him,'' Cassie said firmly. ''But I thought it would be easier to be careful with the door than to close it up altogether and have to use the French doors off the patio.''

''And walk all the way around the complex to get to the parking lot? I'd say so.'' Jake set his briefcase down and shrugged his trench coat off, pausing to rub his shoulder.

He looked tired, Cassie thought, and sore. ''Are you all right? That looks painful.''

''My shoulder? It's just where I hit the door last night.''

''In that case, I won't waste sympathy on you.'' Cassie crossed the foyer and went back to her chair. ''I'd just about made up my mind that you weren't coming…'' Just in time, she swallowed the last word.

But Jake didn't miss a beat as he followed her into the living room. ''Coming home? What a concept.''

I should have expected that, Cassie told herself. *And the irony in his voice, too.*

Still, there was a strange hint of possessiveness in the way he stood in the arched doorway between the foyer and the living room, leaning against the wood frame, every muscle relaxed. ''Why did you think that?'' he asked lazily.

''Because apparently all your stuff was gone.''

"You've been inspecting my quarters, I see. Was that move prompted by curiosity or fear?"

"Neither," Cassie said with as much dignity as she could muster. "I was helping Buddy clear out the contents of the master bath before he started work this morning, and I happened to notice."

Jake shrugged. "You told me to cover up anything I didn't want to get dusty, so I did. Were you worried?"

"That you'd skipped out—without notice, much less taking care of the door? Of course not. I love being in a strange house at night, in a windstorm, with a door that's about as secure as plastic wrap to hold out the bad guys."

"Well, that's a relief."

"What is?"

"That I'm apparently not on your list of bad guys any more."

"Don't get a big head about it," Cassie recommended. "Though you could rise a couple of notches in my estimation if you happen to know anything about taking a cell phone apart." She frowned at the recalcitrant battery cover once more.

"Toss it here." Jake sat down across from her in a big wing chair and dug into his trouser pocket.

"No wonder men wear out their pockets," Cassie muttered as he pulled out a sizeable folding knife and selected a blade. "Our clients could keep a seamstress busy full time, just mending what they rip up." She watched as he pried at the battery cover. "You know, I wouldn't have expected Caleb Tanner to be the slave-driving sort."

Jake glanced at her over the gleaming blade of his knife. "What makes you think he is?"

"Just the fact that you're trailing in at this hour, and you don't look as though you've been at a party. Your first day of work, too."

"You'd be wrong." Jake put the knife down on the coffee table and pressed both thumbs against the battery cover.

"He's not a slave driver?" A sharp crack from her telephone made Cassie sit up straight.

"I *was* at a party. At least, I think that's what it was. Where's the new battery?"

She tossed him the package. "Not one of Caleb's parties, surely, or you'd appear to have enjoyed yourself."

"I thought you didn't know him." Jake snapped the cover into place once more and dropped the cell phone into Cassie's lap.

"I've never met him. But anybody in Denver who's been halfway awake in the last year has heard all about the playboy millionaire and his bimbo of the week." She pressed the phone's power button and watched in delight as the display lit up for the first time since it had died on her in the supermarket aisle that afternoon, in the midst of a call from a client.

"Bimbo, singular?" Jake asked. "From all appearances I'd say he doesn't limit himself to one at a time."

"You could be right about that. The impression I get is that there's usually a main squeeze and a whole lot of ladies-in-waiting. So how many were at Caleb's party?"

"Bimbos? I lost count." He stretched out in the chair with a sigh and closed his eyes.

Cassie eyed him curiously. The pool of light from the floor lamp beside her place on the couch faded to a soft glow as it reached him, and his face was shadowed by the angled back of the wing chair. His eyelashes looked abnormally long and dark and thick in the dim light. He sighed, and his fingertips once more groped for the obviously sore spot on his shoulder.

Concern bloomed deep inside Cassie. If she could help—

The last thing you need to do is start feeling maternal, she ordered. *He did it to himself.*

She pulled a stack of flyers across the table toward her. "What's the matter?" she asked with mock sympathy. "Why wasn't the party any fun? Wouldn't he share the bimbo ration?"

"On the contrary. He was nothing but generous."

"Oh." Too late, Cassie heard the surprised tremor in her voice, and she tried feebly to recover. "Well, no wonder you're tired."

Jake opened one eye and smiled. "Don't fret. No matter how hard he tried, none of them paid any attention to me with Caleb Tanner in the room."

Don't fret? Annoyance at his blithe assumption made Cassie's throat feel hot and tight. "Believe me," she said crisply, "I wasn't brooding over the idea of you with a harem." And it was just as well the picture didn't bother her, she thought, because the denial didn't quite ring true.

She frowned at a flyer while she tried to figure out why the statement had bothered her, and finally she had it. A bimbo, by definition, was a little short of intellectual power. But a woman would have to be lacking a brain altogether to take on a roomful of competitors for the feeble chance of gaining Caleb Tanner's attention when Jake was right there too.

Wait a minute, she told herself. There was something very wrong with the logic of that argument; there was simply no comparison between Jake, the rolling stone who apparently couldn't hold onto a job for more than a few months, and Caleb Tanner the millionaire playboy. Putting them up in competition was hardly fair.

Fair to whom? whispered a tiny voice in the back corner of her mind.

To Jake, of course, she told herself rudely. He couldn't possibly rival someone with Caleb Tanner's advantages.

Are you certain of that? the voice argued.

Cassie pushed the pamphlets away again and got to her feet. "I'm going to make myself a cup of hot chocolate," she heard herself say. "Would you like one?"

Jake murmured something which sounded like sleepy assent, and Cassie retreated to the kitchen. *So much for not being maternal*, she told herself.

Though actually, she argued, it wasn't as if she was giving Jake special treatment. He'd fixed her cell phone, hadn't he? She was just doing him a favor in return. And it was only polite, when she was going for a hot drink for herself, to offer him one as well. She'd do the same for any client, wouldn't she? Or any friend?

Of course, she reminded herself, Jake Abbott fit into neither category.

She came back with a tray and a microwaved hot pack. "Here, put this on your shoulder. Heat will help it."

Jake grinned. "I thought you weren't going to be sympathetic." He sat up and draped the pack into place. "Have you always taken care of people?"

Not always willingly, she almost said. "I suppose so. My mother wasn't well when I was a kid, and there was nobody else to fill in the gaps."

"What about your father?"

He was a lot better at creating gaps than filling them. But Cassie knew it had been only a casual question, certainly not one which called for a complete answer. "He had his own agenda. Anyway, I learned how to do lots of things, and now I do them because I get paid."

"It's an odd sort of job."

Cassie thought that statement was almost funny—coming from a man who'd had a variety of employment. "Just because I don't work at a regular office, with a regular boss, doesn't mean this isn't a real job—or a respectable one."

"That wasn't what I said."

"But you implied it." She smoothed out a rejected pamphlet and with a few swift folds turned it into a paper airplane, then sailed it at him. "See our motto on the back? It's more than just a sales slogan, you know, it's a fact of modern life."

Jake unfolded the pamphlet. "I suppose you mean this bit. *Every working person needs a wife.*"

"It's true, in the sense that every busy individual needs someone who organizes and handles details and makes life a little more manageable. Now that so many women work outside their homes, they need help even more than their husbands do. If they have husbands at all, that is— a lot of our clients are single parents. We fill in the gaps— pick up the pieces—make it possible for them to spend their time doing what they want to do instead of chasing after errands."

Jake looked at her thoughtfully over the rim of his mug. "So who takes care of your details?"

The question took Cassie by surprise; it was the first time anybody had ever asked. "Today, I'd have cheerfully paid one of my partners to go grocery shopping for me."

"Why didn't you?"

"For one thing, they were both already busy. Then, of course, Sabrina doesn't know a chicken breast from a pork chop, so it would be somewhat worse than useless to send her to the supermarket."

"So you run everybody else's errands all day and still have all of yours to do after hours."

"It's not quite that rigid. Lots of times I can cram things together—I can buy a white T-shirt or mail a birthday card or return a library book or pick up a battery for myself while I'm doing a client's business."

"I'll make a mental note to check my grocery store receipt *very* carefully," Jake murmured.

"I didn't mean I run things together financially," Cassie said irritably. Then she saw the twinkle in his eyes, made a face at him, and drawled, "Though of course it was quite a temptation to tell you that you were getting gourmet olives and imported beer when I'd actually bought the generic varieties."

"Generic *beer*?" Jake sounded horrified.

"You mean you'd have noticed? I always thought all beer tasted alike."

"Then you've obviously never tasted the good stuff."

Cassie ignored him. "I could have probably added a couple of dollars to your bill—and my profit—that way. You'll find the receipt on the second shelf of the refrigerator, by the way. It's tucked under the bottle of ketchup."

"Shall I go get the cash right now, or will you trust me till morning?"

"For a small interest charge," Cassie said with mock austerity, "I'll consider letting you put off paying till afternoon."

Jake's eyes lit with delight, and she felt her stomach lurch with the impact of his smile. *This is not good*, she told herself, and almost started laughing at the understatement.

But of course noticing a sexy smile was a whole lot different from falling for its charming owner. And she was in absolutely no danger of doing that.

Cassie took a deep breath. "We're not busy every minute, anyway," she said. "So there are whole days when I can do whatever I want—so long as it includes trying to drum up more clients."

"You mean the world isn't beating a path to your door?"

"Let's just say that not everyone is convinced yet of the value of having a wife on call."

"If it's any comfort, Caleb thinks it's a great idea. Renting a wife instead of making a permanent investment in one, I mean."

Cassie wrinkled her nose in distaste. "With the kind of women he hangs around with, I'm not surprised. Still—" She hesitated.

"You might as well go ahead and say it, Cassie."

"Well—doesn't it bother you? His attitude toward women, I mean?"

"Obviously you think it should."

And just as obviously, Cassie thought, *it hadn't occurred to Jake to develop an opinion.* "I suppose since you're only working for him, it's none of your business. But I've always thought the boss's character was a good indicator of what kind of boss he's likely to be."

"And if he cheats on his wife or his income tax, then he'll probably cheat his employees too. That's interesting," Jake murmured.

"My philosophy, you mean? I suppose you think it's simplistic and naive, but—"

"No. I think it sounds like you've been burned along the way. Was the man you're thinking of dishonest in general, or only where you were concerned?"

Cassie felt herself coloring and tried to fight off the reaction. She certainly wasn't going to confide in Jake Abbott about Stephan. "We were talking about Caleb Tanner," she said firmly.

Jake looked at her for a long time, and then said gently, "Of course we were—if you say so. Caleb and his women. Personally, I think the only important issue there is whether he can keep the women in their proper place and tend to his business—and I'd say, from what I saw tonight, that he doesn't have any trouble with that."

"Good," Cassie said briskly. "I'm glad you're satisfied with his practical outlook." She pushed aside the blanket she'd draped across her lap. "Well, it's getting late, and Buddy will be here first thing in the morning. Which reminds me, he promised me he'd try to find a replacement door."

"I knew you could wrap him around your little finger."

"He said he'd *try*," Cassie repeated. "But of course when I asked him about installing it, he just shifted his toothpick and pointed out that he hadn't allowed any too much extra time for this job as it was, so if I wanted the hot tub in on schedule..."

"I think if Peggy was given the choice—"

"You're betting that she'd rather have a complete front door than her whirlpool? I'm not so sure, myself. For one thing, I didn't know till Buddy started work that she hadn't even moved her extra toothbrush out of the bathroom."

Jake frowned. "I'm sure I'm supposed to make the same kind of great deductions from that fact that you've apparently drawn, but I'll admit it—I'm lost."

"She just left everything right where it was," Cassie said a bit impatiently. "In Buddy's way. I think you're absolutely right that Roger didn't know about this project. I think she's planning to surprise him with the new tub when they get home, so she didn't want to do anything that might make him suspicious—like cleaning all the paraphernalia out of the bathroom."

"And you also think if it isn't done when they get home, there will be hell to pay."

"Maybe not only from Peggy, either. If Roger was in favor of tearing up the bathroom, surely she wouldn't have tried to keep him in the dark about it."

"*If* she's really trying to do it behind his back, instead of just being too lazy to clear out her stuff."

"Whichever it is, she's not going to be pleased at any delay, and that's why I don't think we should pull Buddy off the tub project, even if he was willing. Which he doesn't seem to be."

Jake shrugged. "By the time he finds a door, the tub might be done."

Cassie stopped in the doorway, one foot already in the foyer. "Now *there's* a cheerful thought. I know you said it's an unusual door, but surely it can't be impossible to match."

"How should I know? Buddy mumbled something about it being hard to get replacements once things start getting old."

"This place isn't an antique, Jake."

"No, but it's a long way from brand-new. Anyway, I only meant that the tub project might go so smoothly that he wants the other job to fill in the gap in his calendar."

Cassie's eyes brightened. "I've got it! You could volunteer to help him with the tub. That way he'd end up with oodles of extra time." She frowned. "Or maybe he wouldn't."

"If you're saying that I'd only get in his way and slow him down, I don't think you'd get any argument from Buddy about that."

"You know," Cassie said thoughtfully, "I don't think Buddy likes you."

"So maybe *you* should volunteer to hand him his tools,

instead of trying to sign me up for the job. Even if you got in his way, I'll bet he wouldn't mind."

"You really have an over-active imagination, Abbott. This notion you've got that Buddy's developed a crush on me—"

"Give me one good reason he shouldn't have," Jake challenged.

Cassie's jaw dropped. "That's really unfair, you know. If I give you a reason, I'm running myself down, and if I don't you'll probably say I'm conceited."

"No, I'd tell you that even a guy who thinks a tooth-pick is a fashion accessory is allowed to have good taste in other departments."

Cassie thought it over. "I think that might have been an accidental compliment," she said finally.

"Only it wasn't accidental." Jake took the hot pack off his shoulder and dropped it into his chair, following her into the foyer. "Thanks, Cassie." Casually, he flicked a hand over her hair.

Cassie tried to will herself not to shiver under his touch, but she wasn't entirely successful. *That's the way, Kerrigan*, she told herself ironically. *Go ahead and act like an inexperienced kid who just got her first word of approval from a guy*. She saw him start to smile and said, a little too quickly, "I told you there's a draft in here."

He held out a hand toward the door. "You're right. Want my suggestions for keeping warm tonight?"

"No, thank you," Cassie said crisply. "I think I can imagine what you have in mind. You and Caleb Tanner and your ideas of keeping women in their proper place—"

"All I was going to suggest," Jake murmured, "was that you pile an extra blanket on your bed. But you ob-viously have better ideas, so if you'd like to share—"

Cassie turned on her heel and marched up the stairs, stamping her feet in a vain effort to drown out the warm, rich chuckle which pursued her.

Her hair had been softer than Jake had imagined possible. The tight red curls weren't in the least wiry; instead, each was a silken spiral which twisted naturally around his fingertips, drawing him in. It had taken real effort to pull his hand away instead of plunging deeper into the mass of curls.

He still wasn't certain why he'd backed off. Perhaps it was the way she'd trembled under his touch like a wild bird, half tamed by hunger but still wary of a too-sudden move.

He picked up the hot pack from his chair and gathered up the empty mugs. The Rent-a-Wife flyer Cassie had pitched at him had fallen off the edge of the coffee table; he picked it up to put it back on the stack.

Rent-a-Wife. Caleb Tanner was right; what a delightful, sensible, practical idea it was, to have all the niceties of a woman around the house with none of the drawbacks. No one sitting at home building up expectations. Nobody expecting a man to turn up on time every night, or to remember to call if he was going to be a few minutes late. Nobody to interrupt his work to ask him to bring home a gallon of milk...

Inside the pamphlet was a blank column, obviously intended for the personal notation she'd spoken of. On this one, Cassie had written ''Dear Jake''—and then she'd tried, not entirely successfully, to scribble it out.

So she'd been sitting there thinking about him, had she? Waiting for him?

Jake felt a little curl of anticipation deep inside. His stay in Denver might be only a short one, but there was no reason it couldn't be enjoyable—if Cassie was of the same mind...

What would happen, he wondered, if he went upstairs right now and knocked on her door? She'd shivered when he touched her....

Or maybe it hadn't been because of him at all. She was right, he realized. The damned foyer was like a wind tunnel, and the door sighed and creaked like a haunted house. No wonder Buddy had wanted to block the thing up altogether.

Jake muttered a curse under his breath and dug through the junk drawer in the kitchen till he found a handful of rusty thumb tacks. For tonight, the blanket Cassie had snuggled under in the living room would do to help cut the draft. Tomorrow he'd talk to Buddy about something sturdier. They might have to use the French doors off the living room after all.

By the time he'd fitted the blanket into place to shield the battered door, everything was quiet upstairs. Jake paused for just an instant outside the guest-room door, then shook his head ruefully. Only his own wishful thinking had suggested there had been any kind of invitation in Cassie's actions tonight. Even that tremulous little shiver of hers had a perfectly natural explanation—it was even colder upstairs.

He pushed open the door to the master suite and stopped dead on the threshold. This morning, he had left a bedroom; tonight he was coming back to a carpenter's workshop.

The bathroom door, off its hinges, was propped against the walk-in closet where he'd stored all his things. Behind it a huge mirror leaned against the wall and cast unexpected reflections throughout the room. A pair of sawhorses had been set up on a tarp spread across the center of the carpet, topped with a banged-up chunk of plywood on which stood a line of power tools. Another tarp lay across the bed, piled with boxes of plumbing pipes and connectors. A pair of cabinets that had been pulled out of the bathroom to leave room for the whirlpool were now stacked squarely in the pathway between door and bed. The window stood half-open, with a metal channel rigged up in the opening to carry debris down to the patio below.

No wonder Cassie had complained of the house creaking, of the wind whistling through the foyer. Even with the door closed, air from the open window would have seeped through the crevices, creating the draft downstairs. Now, with the bedroom door open, the brisk, cold breeze whipped a fine gritty dust through the air, stinging Jake's eyes.

He should have listened to her, Jake thought morosely. Cassie had warned him, and he should have paid attention. *I don't think Buddy likes you,* she'd said.

That appeared, Jake thought, to be the understatement of the year.

He picked up one end of the bottom cabinet, trying to move the stack aside far enough so he could at least get to the bed. But he'd underestimated both the weight and the awkwardness of the move, and pain clamored through his shoulder.

At the same instant, a woman's shriek ripped the air.

"What the hell...?" Jake dropped the cabinet and swore as it smashed through the buttery soft leather of his wing-tip shoe and crushed his toes.

And out in the hallway, Cassie shrieked again.

CHAPTER FOUR

JAKE had to lift the cabinet again in order to pull his foot out, and by the time he'd hobbled two steps toward the hallway, Cassie was inside the master bedroom and the door had slammed behind her.

He wasted an instant wondering whether she'd closed it or if the breeze from the window had seized it out of her hand, and then decided there were better things to think about—for instance, Cassie herself.

The nightgown she was wearing was white cotton, almost floor-length, with long sleeves and a high neck and only a hint of decoration. She'd probably bought it, Jake guessed, from her granny's favorite catalog, and she no doubt believed it actually was as all-concealing as the designer had obviously intended it to be.

But the designer hadn't figured on a chilly October breeze which molded the soft cotton around Cassie's body like the flimsiest of togas, making it quite plain that she was wearing nothing underneath.

Jake released a soundless whistle. She might be right, he decided, that Buddy didn't like him—but Jake was beginning to feel very kindly toward the man who'd so helpfully left the window open and provided him with this little show.

"Why are you staring at me?" Cassie asked. She sounded irritated.

Reluctantly Jake shifted his attention to her face. "I'm checking for bruises and bloodstains," he said mendaciously.

"I don't have any."

"That's good." She was pale, he noted, and her eyes were huge and dark, but at least she didn't look as if she could go into shock at any moment. "But you didn't have to make all this fuss, you know. You could have just opened your door and said, 'Oh, Jake, would you like to come in?'"

She glared at him, and the color came back into her face. "I didn't come barging in here because I suddenly got the hots for you, Abbott. I'm here because there's something in the hall bathroom."

"That's more than can be said for the master bath," he murmured, "because all its furnishings have apparently been moved into the bedroom."

"Don't be silly. I mean a—a thing. A live thing."

"That leaves out the possibility of a ghost," Jake mused. "So, do you mean a burglar, or what?"

"I don't know. I just saw eyes. And it moved."

Jake rubbed the bridge of his nose. "It would be helpful if I had a little more information about this intruder," he pointed out.

"It would be *helpful* if you'd do something before he gets to the state line!"

"That wouldn't hurt my feelings a bit," Jake said. "But if you could at least tell me before I go in whether I should tackle high or low—"

"Low. Almost on the floor."

"Oh, good. A midget burglar. Or are we talking about something more the size of a mouse?" The answer was in her eyes, and Jake groaned. "Another thing to add to your list, I see. What was it you told me so blithely that Rent-a-Wife doesn't do? Wash windows, watch babies...or set mousetraps, right?" He strolled down the hall to the bathroom next door to the guest room.

Cassie was right behind him. "You're going in there barehanded?"

Jake flexed his arm in his best circus-strongman style, and winced at the stab of pain in his shoulder. "Do you want to run to the hardware store for a mousetrap at this hour?"

"Not especially."

"And your intruder probably wouldn't be obliging enough to step straight into it, anyway." Jake pushed open the door, flipped on the light, and burst into laughter. "We'll have to get you a lawyer, little guy. Calling you a mouse—she deserves to be sued for slander." He leaned into the shower stall and came out with cupped hands. "Want to see your culprit?"

Cassie backed away. "It's not a mouse?"

"Nope. Just a toad."

She wrinkled her nose. "I'm not sure that's any better. Where did it come from?"

"Up Buddy's wreckage-disposal chute, probably. You can't blame a guy for wanting to be warm and dry on a night like this." *If it had been me, though, I wouldn't have settled for the bathroom*, Jake thought. *Nope, you'd have found me on your pillow.*

"I suppose not." She sounded a little less than certain. "What are you going to do with him?"

"Put him back outside, unless you have a better idea. Want to kiss him and see if he turns into a prince?"

"Wasn't that a frog? Anyway, maybe it's a girl toad."

"Maybe you're wise to hesitate," Jake conceded. "It could actually be Buddy in disguise. There's a real resemblance—the same unblinking stare, the same slow and deliberate moves…"

Cassie shivered.

"Go back to bed," Jake recommended. "At least you

can—your bed isn't full of pipes. It'll take me an hour to clear mine off enough to climb in.''

"You're the one who wanted the master suite, so don't ask for sympathy from me.''

"I wasn't hoping for sympathy,'' Jake assured her. "Now if you'd consider making an offer to share...''

He watched her speedy retreat to the guest room with fascinated interest, because the back view of the simple white nightgown was every bit as superb as the front.

He waited till she'd closed the door before he carried the toad downstairs and relocated him in a corner of the patio where neither wind nor rain would reach him.

After all, Jake thought, it wasn't only Buddy who'd done him a favor tonight. The toad had had a foot in it, too.

Buddy was a few minutes early the next morning, ringing the bell just as Cassie was coming down the stairs. She took one look at the door, rubbed her eyes, and looked again. Yes, there really was a blanket draped not only over the door but concealing the beveled glass panels next to it, casting the foyer into semi-permanent twilight.

She tugged the blanket aside and tried to open the door. The extra weight of the wool made it creak ominously, and Buddy had to duck his head and slide through sideways. "The boss didn't think my fix was good enough, huh,'' he said. It was not a question.

So much for the idea of persuading him to do a permanent repair, Cassie thought. "He put this up because it was awfully chilly in here last night,'' she said hastily. "It had nothing to do with the quality of your work—in fact, he was really pleased with that.''

And why am I explaining, instead of letting Jake stew in his own juice? Cassie sighed. Because the broken door was her problem, too, and it was to her advantage as much as Jake's to keep Buddy happy and cooperative.

"Jake hasn't come down yet," she went on. "Would you like a cup of coffee before you start?"

From the master bedroom came a bellow Cassie thought was worthy of an angry rhinoceros. "Cassie? Why in the devil is my shower disconnected?" Jake appeared at the top of the stairs, a big terry towel wrapped carelessly around his hips. The snowy-white towel made Jake's evenly tanned skin look even more like bronze. "If it's the tub he's working on...Hello, Buddy. What's with the shower?"

Cassie glanced at the man beside her. She could almost feel the tension vibrating through him.

Buddy's voice was tight. "I'm tapping into the shower's water supply to run the feeder lines for the tub, that's why it doesn't work. And it isn't going to work for a few days at least."

So there, he might as well have added, Cassie thought. "Feel free to use my bathroom," she told Jake. "Go easy on my lilac-scented body wash, though, will you? It's the last bottle I've got."

He snorted and vanished down the hall.

By the time Jake appeared in the kitchen, Cassie had heard more than she had ever wanted to know about the various methods of connecting plumbing pipes. As she waited patiently for a break in Buddy's explanation, she couldn't help but notice that Jake didn't smell like lilacs; the scent which drifted across the kitchen toward her was more like juniper. And he hadn't put on a business suit this morning but jeans and a pullover shirt instead.

Surely, she thought, he wasn't going to act on the facetious suggestion she'd made last night that he offer to help Buddy. Was he?

If that was his intention, however, he didn't get the chance to offer his assistance, for Buddy set his empty cup next to the sink and said stiffly, "Thanks for the coffee, ma'am. I'll be getting to my job now, and I'll try my best not to cause any further annoyance." He didn't look at Jake, but it was apparent who he was really talking to.

Buddy's footsteps had hardly died away when Jake said mournfully, "You're right. He doesn't like me."

"Gee, I can't imagine why. Take my advice, Jake, and don't ever buy a house." She let a trace of sarcasm creep into her voice. "Not that I'm going to lie awake nights worrying about it, since I'm sure the idea has never occurred to you."

Jake frowned. "Why shouldn't I?"

"For the sake of the house, that's why. You can't talk to workmen like that. They're a crusty, independent sort, and going around asking stupid questions—"

"Wanting to know why he'd disconnected the shower was not a stupid question."

"And interfering with their work—"

"What are you talking about?"

"Things like hanging up the blanket over the door he'd tried so hard to get back in balance."

"I did that before I realized the hurricane blowing through here was because he'd left a window open upstairs."

"No matter how good the reason, workmen don't stand for amateurs who poke their noses in. You'll be lucky if Buddy doesn't just throw down his tools and walk out— and I'm telling you, Jake, if he does, *you* can explain it to Peggy, because I'm not going to."

"He won't."

Jake sounded so sure of himself that Cassie wanted to

hit him. "Because of your overwhelming charm, no doubt?"

"No, yours. I told you he was suffering from a crush."

"I don't know why you'd think any such thing."

"You disappoint me, Cassie. Didn't you even notice his painfully scraped jaw? He shaved this morning, and I'll bet the rent he didn't do it to impress *me*, sweetheart."

"I didn't pay any attention," Cassie admitted.

"I suppose you didn't realize he put on a clean shirt, either—one that isn't even torn. Poor Buddy. What a waste of time. I suppose next he'll take to outrageous flattery. Though I don't think he's up to the finer flights of poetic expression, so he'd probably settle for something simpler, like saying that you make good coffee. Of course," Jake added, "since I haven't tasted your coffee, I can't judge whether that would actually be flattery or just the simple truth."

"If that's a hint—" She sighed. "I should pour it over your head." She got a mug down from the cupboard.

"You don't have to go that far. Just add it to my account." He wrapped a big hand around the mug and breathed deeply of the scented steam.

"And how are you planning to pay your grocery bill? If you're not going to work today, Jake—"

"What makes you think I'm not?"

"The clothes you're wearing, for one thing."

"This is the approved corporate costume at Tanner Electronics. It's a pretty casual place. In fact, I'll bet half the guys who work there sleep under their desks a good share of the time."

"Well, that would solve the problem of Buddy leaving pipes and faucets on your bed," Cassie mused. "I was actually sort of hoping you'd be around here today."

"You actually want me? Cassie, I hardly know what to say."

Cassie rolled her eyes. "I have a lunch date with my partners, and since Buddy left for a while around noon yesterday, I suppose he'll do the same thing today."

"And you don't want to leave the house empty."

"It isn't that, exactly," Cassie said dryly. "I just don't want to come back to it and find out it's supposed to be empty but isn't."

"That's a nice distinction," Jake admitted. "Maybe I should go see if I can find the toad again and install him as a watchman."

"What good do you think that would do?"

Jake gave her a lazy smile over the rim of his coffee mug. "Well," he said reasonably, "he sent *you* scurrying in a hurry. Didn't he?"

The neighborhood deli where Rent-a-Wife's three partners met each Wednesday for lunch was busier than usual. Cassie was waiting her turn, still trying to decide between pastrami with mustard and roast beef with horseradish, when she spotted Sabrina in the mirror that hung behind the counter.

As Cassie watched, Sabrina stopped just inside the door, took off her dark glasses, and surveyed the room, her exotically slanted green eyes thoughtful. The man standing next to Cassie sighed in half-conscious longing.

The poor goop, Cassie thought. *He's got no idea what's about to hit him.*

Sabrina worked her way through the crowd till she stood beside Cassie and smiled at the man next to her. "Excuse me," she said gently. "I don't mean to be a problem, but you wouldn't mind if I stand here with my friend—would you?"

He mumbled something about being honored, and Sabrina rewarded him with a smile. She turned to link an arm with Cassie's and almost fell into her. "Damn," Sabrina said as she regained her balance. "What did I trip over, anyway?"

"As far as I can tell, a streak of sunshine on the floor tile," Cassie said calmly. "How do you do that, anyway?"

"Fall over a ray of light?"

"No. Make people positively enjoy letting you cut into line."

Sabrina glanced over her shoulder at the man, who was still staring soulfully at her. "Most people," she said very clearly, "are incredibly sweet, when you give them an opportunity to help."

A couple of rows behind them, a matron sniffed.

"It never works for me," Cassie said.

Sabrina glanced at the matron. "You have to practice, darling. So tell me, is he really as good-looking as he sounds on the phone?"

Cassie wanted to groan. Of course Sabrina wouldn't have forgotten hearing Jake yesterday when he'd walked into the kitchen in the midst of Cassie's conversation. "Who?" she parried and stepped up to the counter. "Pastrami on rye with hot mustard, please." She turned back to Sabrina and said pointedly, "You wanted me to come early because you said you had serious business."

"And since it concerns a client, I can't possibly discuss it in a crowded line."

The man at Sabrina's elbow said, "It's your turn, Miss."

Sabrina cast a cool look at the matron behind him and said, "Actually, I believe it's yours. I'm really somewhere there in the back. I just wanted to talk to my friend—

surely you didn't think I'd leap ahead of people who have been waiting?''

The matron sniffed louder. The man stammered. Cassie gathered up her pastrami sandwich and philosophically took a bite.

Sabrina, empty-handed, led the way to a table. "Anyway, what do you mean, *who*? I'm talking about your workman. You can't have forgotten a man who sounds like he does."

Cassie considered trying to explain precisely how she'd acquired a house-mate and decided there was no point. Surely Sabrina couldn't have heard enough on the phone even to recognize Jake's voice if she was to hear it again. Why not let her continue to think it had been Buddy she'd heard instead—and avoid the whole problem of explaining Jake?

"He sounds," Sabrina said, "like a pipe organ with a chest cold."

Cassie choked on her pastrami. "*What* did you say?"

Sabrina shrugged. "You're the poet. I never said I was good at metaphors and images, so don't start acting like you're in literature class again, all right?"

"I'm done with all that. But if I was in the mood to critique, I'd give you credit for originality."

"You're just being sweet. Anyway, I don't have to find just the right turn of phrase because you obviously know exactly what I mean. That low, rumbly voice, with a sexy little throatiness thrown in—"

Sabrina had deduced all that from a couple of sentences half-heard over the telephone? It was the first time Cassie had suspected that Sabrina had the hearing of a lynx. That, she thought, could be dangerous.

As if Cassie had asked the question aloud, Sabrina said, "I called the townhouse to see if you'd bring me a stack of our new flyers. I must have just missed you, because he said you'd only been gone a few minutes.''

There was now no doubt in Cassie's mind that it hadn't been Buddy who'd talked to Sabrina on the phone. She put down her sandwich and was just opening her mouth—without a clue as to what she was going to say—when she spotted a petite blonde at the door. ''There's Paige,'' she said with relief. ''It appears that everyone's running early today. She looks a little distracted, don't you think?''

Sabrina glanced over her shoulder. ''Paige always looks distracted. Sometimes she even looks helpless and fluffy. Of course underneath she's about as fluffy as a pit bull, but for people who don't know that...'' She stood up. ''I'll go get into line legitimately now, and leave you to think over how much you're going to admit about your workman.''

By the time the two of them came back, Cassie had half-consciously shredded her sandwich. Sabrina looked at it knowingly, but before she could comment, Cassie said, ''How's your mother, Paige?'' It wasn't just a distraction technique, she told her conscience; anything which affected her partners—her best friends—was important to her, and so she was naturally concerned about Eileen McDermott.

Paige's forehead wrinkled. ''Apparently she's got a little upper respiratory congestion she didn't tell me about.''

''It's awfully early in the season for that, isn't it? After what happened last winter, no wonder you look distracted.''

Sabrina nodded. ''Pneumonia's nothing to toy with.''

Paige's distant, worried look twisted Cassie's heart, and she fumbled for a way—however feeble—to relieve her partner's pain. ''Tell her if she needs a break from answering Rent-a-Wife's phones to call me," she offered. "I'm going to be stuck in the townhouse till the door's fixed at least, so I might as well be doing something constructive."

And it looked as if Jake wasn't going to be much help at relieving her of duty, she mused. Though he'd kept his word about staying in the house while she was at lunch, he hadn't shown up till the last possible moment, when Buddy had already gone and Cassie was ready to walk out.

"What do you mean, door?" Paige asked. "I thought the whole thing was about a bathtub."

Cassie could have bitten her tongue off.

"Anyway, my mother's chest cold isn't what's bothering me," Paige went on. "It's Rent-a-Wife. I've been adding up the accounts receivable."

"People owe us too much money?" Sabrina asked.

Paige shook her head. "Not exactly. They don't owe us nearly enough right now, because we simply haven't been doing as much business as usual. Cash flow is going to be an even worse problem than normal in the next couple of months. We'll be all right after Christmas, if we have the usual upswing in business with the holidays. But until then..."

"We'll just have to cut down on what we're drawing for living expenses." Cassie knew she sounded calmer than she felt. Trimming back was easier said than done, for all of them. She had student loans to repay. Sabrina had just replaced the transmission in her car, and Paige's mother's monthly pharmacy bills were enormous.

"I've got it," Sabrina said. "Let's take in a new partner."

Paige frowned. "You can't be thinking straight. The problem isn't that we don't have enough hands, or enough time to fill all our customers' requests. It's that we don't have enough business just now to keep the three of us truly busy. If we add another partner, we'll just make things worse.''

"I'm not suggesting we take on just anyone," Sabrina murmured. "I'm talking about Cassie's workman. I suspect a lot of women would pay premium prices to rent a husband who's half as good as he sounds.''

"Believe me," Cassie said, *"he's* only half as good as he sounds—at best. And if you think you can talk him into solving our cash-flow crunch by buying into the partnership, forget it. The man still owes me for two cans of olives, a bottle of ketchup, and a six-pack of beer.''

"A fondness for real food can be acquired," Sabrina said. "You'll just have to work on this one, Cassie.''

"I'd sooner work on the chain gang.''

"If you two would be serious," Paige suggested, "we might be more likely to get somewhere.''

Cassie sobered. "Sorry, Paige. We've got a good mailing list right now. I'll get my share of those flyers out in the next couple of days, and maybe that will drum up some business.''

"If it gets down to the wire," Sabrina said, "I'll ask my father for a loan.''

In the sudden silence which followed, Cassie stared across the table. Sabrina's lips were tight, her jaw was set hard, and her eyes held a determined glitter.

"I'd sooner starve than let you do that," Cassie said frankly.

"Me, too," Paige muttered. "So let's all go back to work and see if we can keep it from getting that bad.''

On the sidewalk just outside the deli, Sabrina dropped into step beside Cassie. "Now I really have to pick up those flyers, and since I still need to talk to you about that client..."

Only someone who knew her as well as Cassie did could tell that Sabrina's smile fell short of its usual radiance. But then, Cassie told herself, from the few things Sabrina had let drop about her father, the thought of going to him with hat in hand could take the glow out of a perfect sunset, much less an ordinary human being.

Sabrina went on, cheerfully, "I guess that means I'll just have to stop by the townhouse and meet your workman after all."

"Don't hold me responsible if you're disappointed," Cassie recommended.

"Why are you trying so hard to keep my hopes low?" Sabrina's eyes opened wide, in mock-amazement. "Cassie, darling—what kind of a friend do you think I am? Surely you don't suspect I'd try to scoop him up, right under your nose?"

You wouldn't have to try, Cassie thought. That was the trouble. It wasn't only men in deli lines who reacted to Sabrina like iron filings to an electromagnet—standing at attention and quivering eagerly each time the current fluctuated.

And what do you care? she asked herself rudely as she drove toward the townhouse. She wasn't worried about Sabrina; she knew from experience that her partner could take care of herself. And if Jake Abbott got his fingers burned—well, he wouldn't be the first man Sabrina had taught a lesson, and it might just do him some good.

In fact, she told herself with steely determination, it could be fun to watch.

It didn't occur to Cassie till she turned the corner nearest the townhouse that Jake might not even be there. Her lunch had run longer than she'd expected; by now Buddy would probably be back, and with him creating more noise and dust than she'd thought possible in the master bathroom, Jake would probably have seized the excuse to go back to whatever it was he'd been doing all morning.

As she pulled into the parking lot, she spotted a figure standing on a ladder which had been propped on the front steps of the townhouse. Buddy, she told herself. He'd gotten the door, thank heaven, and he was installing it....

But the thought wasn't yet fully formed before she knew it wasn't Buddy on the ladder. The man was too tall and not at all lanky, and his short dark hair was ruffling softly in the breeze, not tied back in a tight, greasy ponytail.

Sabrina's vintage convertible pulled into the spot next to Cassie's. "On the other hand," Sabrina murmured as she stepped onto the sidewalk where Cassie waited, "a sight like that is enough to make even the most ethical of people waver in their determination to stay true to their friends."

"As if it matters what you do," Cassie said. "All you have to do is breathe and men fall over themselves. Just look at the way he's staring—and you haven't even smiled at him yet."

Jake was leaning forward on his ladder, arms folded across the top rung, a screwdriver held loosely in one hand, watching their approach. He looked bemused.

And he thought Buddy looked silly, Cassie thought, *because he was drooling over me*. She supposed it all came down to a matter of degree; women like Sabrina attracted the Jakes of the world, while Cassie got the Buddys.

Jake raised the screwdriver in a careless salute and turned his attention back to a bracket he was fastening into place above the door frame. "Did you bring me a sandwich, Cassie?"

"You didn't ask me to," she pointed out.

"Honey, you need to work on your conscience—develop one, I mean. This morning you didn't even notice Buddy's clean shave and new shirt, then you ignored my gaunt and starving expression..."

"Yeah, you look hardly strong enough to drive a screw," Cassie jeered. "What are you doing, anyway?"

"Putting up a security camera."

"Why?"

"So you'll feel secure."

"Oh. You mean I can sit in the living room and watch on the television screen while somebody breaks down the feeble remains of this door."

"Or, when you come back and find the place ravaged, you can check out whether it was bad guys, a strong breeze, or just your favorite toad coming to call."

"Isn't this something of a waste of time? I mean, even if it takes a few days to get the new door—"

Jake gave the screwdriver a final twist. "I plan to leave the camera for Peggy and Roger, so the next time somebody swipes their extra key, they'll be able to check the tape and see who it was."

Cassie decided it wasn't worth her while to point out that in fact nobody had taken the key; Jake would probably just remind her that it was in her possession and he still didn't have one. "I hope you checked out this idea with Buddy before you started."

"I couldn't possibly do anything that would make me any more unpopular with Buddy."

Sabrina had been standing absolutely still, except for turning her head to follow the conversation. "Who's Buddy?"

"The contractor," Cassie said.

Sabrina moved a step forward and smiled brilliantly up

at Jake. Her toe caught on the leg of the stepladder, and it rocked perilously for an instant. "Sorry," she said. "I seem to be having a very clumsy day. Then you must be...?" Her voice trailed off invitingly.

"Not Buddy," Jake said coolly.

Cassie's eyebrows rose. "Goodness," she said mildly. "You must be hungry to start snapping like that. I could make you an olive-and-ketchup sandwich, if you'd like." Without waiting for an answer, she ducked around the ladder and through the half-open door into the townhouse. At least, she noticed, the blanket was gone.

Sabrina followed, looking thoughtful.

"I warned you," Cassie said. "Though I'm a little surprised myself."

"Well, I did almost knock the man off his ladder." Sabrina riffled through the stack of pamphlets, still piled on the coffee table, and tucked a bundle into her handbag. "About this client situation," she began.

"You mean there really is one? It wasn't just an excuse to meet Jake?"

"Jake," Sabrina said softly. "What a nice name. And you say it with such a special note in your voice, too."

"Who's the client, Sabrina?"

Suddenly serious, Sabrina sat down on the edge of a chair. "Ben Orcutt. You've done some work for him, haven't you?"

Cassie shivered. "Yeah. And if he wants his refrigerator cleaned out again, tell him to call the hazardous waste disposal team."

"That bad, huh? I was supposed to be balancing his checkbook yesterday, but he asked while I was there if I'd just sew a couple of buttons back on shirts for him. And don't look at me that way," Sabrina said defensively. "I got the job done."

"How many times did you stab yourself with the needle?"

"Three."

"Is that total, or per button?"

"I did not come here to discuss buttons," Sabrina said with dignity. "I wanted to talk about what Ben was doing while I was sewing. Has he ever...acted strangely while you were there?"

"Ben's been strange from the day he was born. Which is at least seventy-nine years ago, right?"

"More like sixty-five, I think. And that's not what I meant. He didn't actually make a pass. I almost wish he had, because I could have handled that. He was just so overwhelmingly friendly that I thought—"

"That he was thinking about it?"

"Exactly. Has he ever acted that way around you?"

"Men don't tend to lose their perspective over short redheads the way they do over women like you. Though now that you mention it—yeah, *overwhelmingly friendly* describes it pretty well."

"So what do we do about it? I mean, we can't have the clients ambushing us in the pantry." She shot a sideways look at Cassie. "Though I'll bet if it had been you instead of me, and Jake instead of Ben Orcutt, you'd have knocked over the cans of creamed corn in your rush to—"

"Jake is not a client," Cassie said firmly.

"Well, that certainly makes things easier."

Cassie decided to ignore her. "Have you talked to Paige about this?"

"Are you kidding? Paige already thinks there isn't one man in the western hemisphere who has decent judgment about anything. Give her half a reason and she'd try to declare male clients off limits altogether. And then the cash flow would really be in the soup." Sabrina stood up.

"I don't expect you to have answers, Cassie—but I had to tell somebody. I was starting to think I might be imagining things."

Cassie walked her to her car, noting that Sabrina stepped very carefully around the ladder still partially-blocking the doorway.

As she got into her convertible, Sabrina unfolded her sunglasses and paused with them halfway onto her nose. "By the way, Cassie," she asked earnestly. "I almost forgot. Do I want to hear the story about the toad?"

CHAPTER FIVE

As Cassie reached the front steps once more, Jake leaned down from the ladder. "Would you hand me the camera from that box?"

She passed it up to him and watched as he struggled to connect it to the bracket. He still seemed to be favoring his shoulder, she thought.

"If I ever lose my mind enough to buy a house," he said finally, "I'm going to take your advice."

"My advice was not to make the purchase in the first place," Cassie pointed out.

"I mean your standard advice. I'll rent a full-time wife to go with it. Then someone like you can deal with things like this."

"And the wallpaper, too?"

He looked down at her with obvious foreboding. "All right—I know better than to ask you to break it to me gently. What about the wallpaper?"

"On the foyer wall. When you kicked the door in, the splinters ripped the paper. I just noticed it this morning, but I'll guarantee Peggy will spot it within five minutes after she gets home."

Jake shrugged and gave the mounting screws a last twist.

"So what are you planning to do about the wallpaper?"

"Not waste time worrying about it, that's sure. I'll probably tell her to have new paper hung and send me the bill."

"Do you have any idea what that's likely to cost?"

77

Cassie didn't wait for an answer, because numbers were ticking through her head. "I wonder who she'll have do the job?"

"I don't know, and I don't care."

"I don't suppose you'd suggest Rent-a-Wife?"

"Sure. At least it'll be some consolation—the money will be going to a good cause." He reached for a cable which dangled from a small hole drilled through the wall. "There should be a connector somewhere in the box."

Cassie scrabbled through the packing materials till she found it. "Aren't you glad I'm here so you don't have to climb down every time you need something?"

"I'd climb down willingly if your friend was still hanging around."

Well, that's no surprise, Cassie thought. *I knew that snappiness of his didn't have anything to do with Sabrina.* "I suppose next you're going to ask me for her phone number."

"I wasn't planning to."

He sounded perfectly matter-of-fact, as if he'd thought it all out—and that was what made Cassie suspicious. "Why not?" she demanded. "Don't you think I'd give it to you?"

Jake leaned on the top rung of the ladder, the cable dangling negligently from his hand. "Of course you would," he said gently. "Because if you didn't, you think I might suspect you of being selfish."

"Selfish?" Cassie sputtered. "Because I don't want to share you, I suppose!"

"Of course," Jake mused. "Though I didn't expect you to admit it so easily. Give me one more minute and I'll come down so you can tell me nicely—"

"I was not making a statement, Abbott."

"Are you sure about that? You didn't have to stop and think about it long."

"I was merely pointing out what a stupid assumption you were making."

Jake shrugged. "Whatever you say. In any case, Caleb probably already has her phone number."

Cassie was bewildered by the sudden tangent. Wouldn't it be easier—and far more sensible—to ask her rather than his boss? And what made him think Sabrina knew Caleb Tanner any more than Cassie herself did? Then the light dawned, and her blood started to sizzle. "Wait a minute. If you're suggesting that Sabrina is the kind of bimbo Caleb Tanner likes to hang around with—"

"She certainly has the looks for the part."

Cassie was fairly certain he didn't mean it as a compliment. "And a first-class brain to go with it."

"Which no doubt accounts for why she's driving a ten-year-old car and working for an outfit like Rent-a-Wife."

Cassie bristled. "That car is a collector's item. And at least Sabrina and I know where we'll be employed next month." *But maybe not a lot longer than that*, a little voice whispered, *because if the cash flow situation doesn't improve in a hurry...*

"Meaning that I don't. Well, that's true enough."

Cassie could detect nothing in his voice except good humor, but she felt a little ashamed of herself for pointing out the obvious. "Anyway, take my word for it—Sabrina has a whole lot more going for her than her looks."

I can't believe I'm doing this, she thought. The last thing Sabrina needed was another hanger-on, so why in heaven's name was Cassie trying to encourage Jake to be one? Of course, anything was better than having him think Cassie herself was eager for his attention.

Aren't you? her conscience whispered. *And as for that*

zealous defense of your partner—could there have been just a little relief mixed in with the loyalty?

"I notice you didn't mention grace as one of her assets," Jake said thoughtfully. "Is she always that clumsy?"

"No," Cassie jeered. "I'm sure she tripped over the ladder on purpose, just to get your attention. You know, Jake, you're the most conceited and arrogant male I've ever had the misfortune to run into."

He checked the cable connection and descended from the ladder. "At any rate, that's why I said I'd climb down if she was still here. Not because I was dying to get better acquainted with her, but because I didn't want to die by getting knocked off a ladder."

"It *would* sound silly in the obituary," Cassie murmured.

Jake gave her a sideways look as he folded up the ladder and set it to one side of the front door. "Come in and let's make sure this thing works."

"I still don't know why you're bothering with this. If Buddy can find a replacement any time soon—"

He pushed the door wide. "I suppose you like the idea of being stuck sitting here day after day while he looks for one."

"Now that you mention it, no. How kind of you to think of that, Jake." It was true, as far as it went, and Cassie tried very hard to keep the irony in her voice to a minimum. "It's incredibly thoughtful of you to buy me a little freedom."

"Isn't it?" Jake sounded quite proud of himself. "I can think of a number of ways you could show me how grateful you are, Cassie."

She hadn't realized before how small the foyer was,

how cramped and airless. Or was it just the intensity of Jake's gaze that made it hard for her to breathe?

She managed to put a smile in her voice. "You're nothing but an opportunist, Jake. You may as well admit that you put the camera in purely to release yourself from house-sitting duty. Didn't you?"

"Of course," he said easily. "But I thought if you were looking for an excuse, it would be to my advantage to help you find one. Just in case you wanted to do something like this."

His hands cupped her face, turning it up to his. As he leaned closer, his fingers slid into her hair, tangling in the tight curls.

Apart from his fingertips almost massaging her scalp, he wasn't touching her at all—but Cassie's entire body tingled with awareness. When his mouth brushed hers with the gentleness of a butterfly's wing, every cell of her body vibrated with the need for more. She gave a little sigh and closed her eyes and waited.

But he didn't deepen the kiss, or pull her tight against him. He let her go instead, and when he raised his head, Cassie wanted to groan with pain at the idea that he'd been able to stir her so deeply and remain unmoved himself.

Then she saw how dark his eyes had grown, and warmth bloomed deep inside her. "If I ever do want to do something like that," she said huskily, "I'll remember that I have a handy excuse."

A smile tugged at his mouth. "You do that, Cassie." He pulled open the door of the closet which was tucked under the stair landing, just inside the front door, and fiddled with a tiny television set.

She was still breathing a little too fast, but she tried to

sound completely normal. "You put the monitor in the closet?"

"Nobody's going to look for it among the boots. Besides, if I'd strung a cable across the width of the house, Peggy might not have been too happy with me."

"Especially if you'd hung it from the picture hooks. And you really don't think she'll object to the hole you've drilled in her front wall?"

"I don't see why. When I tell her she's part of a marketing survey for Tanner Electronics, free to suggest improvements in the product..."

"I didn't know they made security systems." Cassie took a closer look. "So that's why you got a sudden attack of handy-man-itis, you're trying out the products. Is that what you're doing for Caleb Tanner? Marketing research?"

"I do a lot of things."

"Is your official title a state secret or something?" Cassie asked irritably. "I was only making conversation, asking how the job's going. Fine, you say? Glad to hear it. How many bimbos were on site this morning?"

"Three or four. And I'm not sure how it's going. At first glance it looks like controlled chaos, but on closer inspection..."

"You're not sure if control or chaos will win out?"

"Or which side of the equation Caleb's on." He leaned toward the monitor. "This is too small to really see anything."

"A bigger monitor wouldn't fit in the closet. Maybe if you just distract the bimbos for a while, you can see what Caleb's really up to."

Jake looked intrigued. "That's an idea. I hope my eyes aren't deceiving me, but see here." He pointed at the screen.

Cassie bent closer. "Looks like the mailman's delivering a super-sized greeting card. No, wait—it's a door. Poor Jake, you did all this work for nothing. Buddy found a..." Her voice trailed off in shock as the man outside set down his burden and turned to ring the bell.

It was Buddy, all right. But the change in him since he'd left the townhouse shortly before noon was incredible.

"Maybe he likes you better than I thought he did, Jake," Cassie managed to say. "Because that's your haircut he's wearing all of a sudden."

"I should no doubt be honored." Jake opened the door.

"Where do you want me to put this?" Buddy asked.

Cassie leaned against the old, patched-together frame. "How about in this opening right here?"

Buddy shook his head. "Can't. It all has to be painted first. And it can't go in the old casing anyway, because the whole unit has to be replaced. You're lucky as it is that those glass pieces next to it were put in completely separate, so at least all you have to replace is the door."

Cassie looked over his shoulder at the new door. The wood-grained panel was the same sickly beige as a still-frozen turkey carcass—and about as inviting.

"I can try to find someone to do the painting," Buddy said, "but I can't promise when they'll get around to it."

"It can't be that big a job," Cassie protested.

"Not exactly. But it's time-consuming, and it takes up lots of room. The door has to be laid out flat so the paint doesn't run, and one side has to dry completely before you can flip it to do the other one. Lots of people don't want to bother with little stuff like this."

So much for the idea that the problem was solved, Cassie thought. She glanced speculatively at Jake. "What do you plan to do now?"

"At the moment, nothing except thank Buddy and ask for the bill," he said. "I have to go back to work. And since I've taken such a long lunch hour, it'll probably be too late when I get out of there to stop at a paint store tonight, so if…"

"That figures," Cassie grumbled.

"But you can go out to buy paint with confidence," Jake pointed out helpfully, "because the house is safe now, with the camera running all the time."

Cassie gave in. "All right, I'll go get the paint. But I'm putting the time on your bill."

Jake's brows drew together. "Don't I get any kind of kickback for funneling the wallpaper job your way? Of course, if you have other payment terms in mind besides money…"

His gaze slid slowly over Cassie, heating every square inch of skin and burning up her voice.

Obviously in no hurry, Jake completed his survey, picked up his briefcase and strolled down the sidewalk toward his car.

Buddy looked after him with what Cassie might have called black loathing, if her perceptions hadn't been colored by her own irritation. Bad enough to make that kind of insinuation, she thought, but to do it in front of an audience…what was he trying to do, anyway? Prod Buddy into some sort of competition?

"Where am I supposed to put the door?" Buddy asked again.

"How about on the patio? There's sort of a roof to protect it."

"Too much dust, in the open air. It'll ruin the finish if you try to paint it out there."

"I never said I was going to be the one to paint it."

Cassie sighed. "I suppose the living room, then. It's the only space that's big enough."

Buddy carried a set of sawhorses and a tarp down from his work area and started to take the door off the hinges.

Cassie, guiltily feeling that the man deserved some acknowledgement of the extra work he was doing, went to get him a cold soda.

When she came back, Buddy had set the casing up against a bookshelf in the corner and arranged the door in the center of the living room, balanced on the sawhorses as if it were a table top so it would be ready to paint.

Cassie stopped on the threshold, startled by how big the thing had suddenly grown. One corner of the panel butted almost against the baby grand, while the opposite one overhung the coffee table. The only apparent way to get from one side to the other was to walk out the French doors to the patio and around the entire complex to the front entrance. "Or possibly just do the limbo between the sawhorses," she muttered.

"Ma'am?"

"Nothing. I'm just frustrated when I get stuck with a mess, especially when I didn't do anything to cause the damage in the first place. I won't even be able to work in here now."

Buddy frowned. "I guess it's none of my business..."

You can say that again, Cassie thought, but she followed the rule she'd set out for Jake just this morning and bit her tongue. Letting Buddy have his say wouldn't hurt anything. When a man had done the kind of favors Buddy had, it wouldn't hurt to listen to him; it didn't mean she had to agree. Cutting him off, on the other hand, was practically guaranteed to lead to resentment and even more problems down the road.

"And I don't hold with kicking in doors," Buddy went on. "But I do see the man's point. Since you locked him out, what else could he do?"

Cassie's jaw dropped. "Is that what he told you happened? We had a fight and I locked him out?"

Buddy looked confused. "You mean that isn't the way it was?"

"Not even close. Mr. Macho Abbott just had to prove—" Fury burned up her voice, and she stalked across the foyer and with her bare hands ripped loose a shred hanging from the door. "I'm going to see if I can match this color," she announced.

And when she got home, she vowed, she was going to drown Jake Abbott in teal-blue paint.

The door of Caleb Tanner's office was standing open when Jake went in that afternoon, but there were no bimbos in sight. Of course, Jake thought, that was probably because Caleb wasn't there, either.

He sat down in an armchair, elbows propped and hands tented under his chin, to think while he waited for the boss to show up. But he had trouble keeping his mind on the question of business when the scent of lilacs kept tickling his nose.

His hands smelled like Cassie, he realized. He must have picked up the scent from her hair, running his fingers through her curls—and the sensible, business-like thing to do would be go to the washroom and scrub it away.

But washing off the scent wouldn't make the thought go away. So he didn't move.

He hadn't quite expected that fleeting kiss to pack such a punch. He'd intended it to be just enough of a taste to intrigue her. As it had, of course—she'd tried mightily to conceal it, but the huskiness in her voice, the slightly unfocused gaze, were impossible to hide.

What he hadn't expected was how he'd reacted. He'd always known Cassie Kerrigan was a nice little package. But he hadn't realized, even last night when he'd gotten an eyeful of that revealing nightgown, that she was a neatly wrapped hunk of dynamite. Another few moments—or if she had taken just the half step which would have brought her tight against his body—and he wouldn't have been able to restrain himself from taking more. Much more.

But if he was careful how he played his cards, the next time he wouldn't have to restrain himself. Because, if he was careful how he played his cards, she wouldn't want him to...

It was past time to devote his attention to figures, he told himself. And he didn't mean Cassie Kerrigan's, either—no matter how clear the picture of that nightgown was in his head.

When Caleb finally came in, he wasn't alone, and the man with him was talking so fast that Caleb could barely acknowledge Jake's presence. He sat on the corner of his desk and listened.

Since Jake hadn't been asked to leave, he stayed in his chair. Without a hint of background, he could pick up only pieces of the conversation—something about a new twist on spring-powered motors. Caleb eventually said, "Fine. Take the time and resources you need to look into it, but get back to me as soon as there's any progress to report."

Despite the fact that he'd comprehended only half the conversation, Jake felt his eyebrows raising.

The engineer left, and Caleb moved from the corner of his desk to the chair behind it.

Jake asked, "Out of idle curiosity, do you have any idea how much money you just told him to spend?"

"Research and development isn't cheap. And since only a few ideas ever pan out, I don't even try to keep track of what each one costs. I have enough trouble keeping track of everything we're looking at." He leaned back and closed his eyes. "I told you all that money stuff wasn't my strong point, anyway."

"Yeah. I'm beginning to realize that."

Caleb sat up with a sigh. "What can I do for you today, Jake?"

"I wanted to run some numbers by you." Jake paused, and then said, "What's on your mind, anyway? If it's business, you'd better tell me what it is. If it's fixable, I'll work on it with you. If it's not, far better that I know it up front instead of finding out later."

"It doesn't have anything to do with the numbers you're working on. It's staff. I've never had trouble hanging onto my people, but lately it seems a bunch of them have taken other jobs."

"What's your definition of a bunch?"

"Four or five."

Jake shrugged. "That doesn't sound like many. There's always a certain amount of turnover—people who get tired of waiting for their chance at fame and fortune and decide to seek it somewhere else." But even as he spoke, he found himself wondering. He'd thought this group was as contented as any he'd ever seen. They'd appeared to be devoted employees, the kind—as he'd told Cassie— who regularly slept under their desks in order to devote more time to their work.

"I just got a resignation letter from one of my best engineers," Caleb said. "And he's leaving at the end of the week, not even giving a full month's notice."

Was this simply a reflection of the ordinary pattern of business? There was no way any employer could keep every single qualified employee, particularly gifted ones such as Caleb was talking about. They were in demand all over, actively courted by other companies.

Or was it worse than that? Was this a case of rats deserting the ship, knowing—subconsciously perhaps—that Tanner Electronics had already passed its prime?

"Have you talked to them?" Jake asked.

"Sure. I've called every one of them in and tried to grill them. Didn't find out anything."

"Maybe the questions were too obvious. This engineer, for instance. If you were to take him out after work tonight…"

"Buy him a few beers, then pop the leading questions."

"Exactly."

"Trouble is, we haven't exactly been in the habit of bellying up to the bar together," Caleb said.

"Make it a going-away party, then. Pick a nice place and invite some other people, maybe ones from his department. Take them to dinner, where he can't just walk away. In a more social atmosphere—"

"*You* could ask the questions," Caleb pointed out. "And you'd be more likely to get answers."

The door was still open, and just outside Jake spotted, from the corner of his eye, the same blonde bimbo who'd been in the office yesterday.

"I came to deliver your sweater, Caleb darling," Angelique said. "It's all finished." She strolled across the room with the exaggerated gait of a model on the runway and set a box in front of Caleb. "And of course I couldn't help overhearing what you were talking about. I'd be happy to plan your party—you know I'm always anxious to help.''

Caleb said, ''What we were talking about isn't exactly your kind of party, Angelique.''

She gave a trill of a laugh. ''Anything you're doing is my kind of party, darling.''

Jake couldn't quite restrain a snort.

She turned to him, eyes wide. ''And who shall I invite for you, Jake dear? I thought you and Missa hit it off especially well last night, and I'm sure she'd cancel her plans if you wanted her to come to a party.''

It was news to Jake that he'd hit it off especially well with anyone last night. He rather thought Missa must be the one who'd reminded him of a well-trained circus horse...

''Dinner at the Pinnacle,'' Angelique decreed. ''It's the best place in town, and the maitre d' owes me a couple of favors, so I'm sure we can still get reservations for tonight. Caleb, darling—how many of us will there be?''

Before they knew it, Jake told himself, the evening would be Angelique's kind of party after all, and nothing would be accomplished. What devil had inspired him to use the word *party*, anyway? If he'd called it a conference, Angelique would probably have ignored the whole idea. But now that she'd shoe horned her way in, it was going to be impossible to dislodge her. He might as well try to distract ants from a picnic lunch.

Distract. What was it Cassie had said about that?

Maybe if you just distract the bimbos for a while, you can see what Caleb's really up to, that was it. And perhaps, as a bonus, he could get a little useful information about what was making Tanner's employees restless, too.

''Thanks anyway,'' Jake said crisply. ''But I'll be bringing a date.''

Dinner at the Pinnacle, he thought. The best place in town. Cassie would no doubt be pleased.

Cassie had moved her stack of pamphlets to the breakfast bar in the kitchen, and she was licking envelopes while she listened to the tense voice at the other end of the telephone. "It's the insurance papers that are getting me down," the woman said. "It was bad enough to lose my mother, but I had no idea how much work and stress would be involved in cleaning out her house and getting it ready to sell. And the bills are still coming from her last stay in the hospital. It's not the money, it's the paperwork. I can't concentrate well enough even to sort it out, much less understand what's been paid—"

"We can take care of all of that," Cassie soothed. "All you have to do is bundle all the papers into a box, and I'll pick it up tomorrow and get started on the insurance. Then we can set a time for all of us to meet at the house, and once you've pointed out the things you want to keep, Sabrina and Paige and I will take care of sorting out the rest and getting it off to charity or auction or wherever you want."

The client sounded pathetically grateful. "You know, I feel like such an idiot," she said, "because most of the time I don't even know what I want to do. But—"

"Under ordinary circumstances, you'd be fine, Jayne. But every knickknack or piece of paper you pick up reminds you of your loss. It's no wonder you're paralyzed just now. Let us help."

"That's it," said the client. "You've hit it exactly. Oh, Cassie, what a relief it is to have someone who understands!"

And what a relief it is, Cassie thought as she put down

the phone, *to have a client with enough work to keep all three of us busy for a week or more.*

She was punching in Paige's cell phone number, eager to tell her the good news, when she heard the characteristic creak of the front door. Probably just Buddy going out to his truck for tools or supplies, she thought. From what Jake had said, he wouldn't be home—to use the term very loosely—for hours yet.

Paige picked up her phone at precisely the same moment that Jake strolled into the kitchen. He smiled at her, ran a careless fingertip from the point of one of her shoulders across the nape of her neck to the other shoulder, and opened the refrigerator door.

The smile and touch made Cassie's heart roll over—and fired up her irritation even more.

"Hello?" Paige repeated.

"Sorry," Cassie said breathlessly. "I'll talk to you later."

"But *you* called *me*," Paige was saying as Cassie hung up.

"There was no need to interrupt your call," Jake said. "My good news can wait."

He certainly sounded cheerful, Cassie thought. And sure of himself, too—as though she'd ended her call because of her enthusiasm to be with him. She'd fix that delusion in a hurry, she decided.

"Well, what I have to say to you can't wait," she said firmly. "How on earth could I possibly have locked you out, when I didn't even know you wanted *in*?"

He stood dead still, holding the refrigerator door open. "What are you talking about?"

"You told Buddy you kicked the door in because I'd locked you out."

Jake's forehead cleared. "Oh. Did I?"

Cassie's fury threatened to choke her. "You don't even know what you told him?"

"No doubt at the time I thought how it happened was none of his business. His part in the mess was fixing it."

"You made it sound like some kind of lovers' spat!"

"I'm not big on the spat part, but—"

"Don't even suggest being lovers."

"I thought it was a great idea," Jake said plaintively. "Come on, Cassie—is it really such a big deal, whatever I said to Buddy? It was actually pretty close to the truth. I *was* locked out."

"If that's what you call the truth, Jake Abbott—"

She saw his gaze shift to the hallway behind her, and looked over her shoulder to where Buddy was standing. His face was expressionless and his voice almost flat. "I'm leaving for the day."

"Would you lock the door on your way out, please?" Cassie asked automatically.

"She has a thing about locks, you know," Jake murmured.

Without a word, Buddy retreated down the hall.

Cassie glared. "You don't have to go making things worse!"

"I'll bet you're really mad at me because Buddy thinks you're some kind of virago instead of the goddess he'd pictured," Jake said.

Cassie reached blindly for something to throw at him and knocked over a cup of stale coffee. Jake jumped for a towel, and by the time they'd mopped up the mess and wiped the splashes off the top few envelopes she'd so painstakingly addressed, Cassie was feeling a little subdued.

Perhaps she had leaped a little too hard on the whole episode. Did it really matter so much, whatever he'd told

Buddy? Had Buddy even gotten it right? And wouldn't she have been just as annoyed if Jake had passed on every detail?

She was propping up the last of the pamphlets to dry, and Jake was wringing out the coffee-soaked towel when the phone rang. Cassie put her hand on it and hesitated.

"Go ahead and answer," Jake said. "I told the playboy millionaire you're my answering service, so he'll be expecting you."

But the voice on the other end of the line wasn't Caleb, it was breathy and affected and emphatically feminine—and in search of Jake.

Cassie handed the phone over to him. "If Miss Sultry Voice there is anywhere near as sexy as she sounds…" *Then you're no competition*, she told herself.

And that was just fine with her. Just because Jake seemed to think an affair would be fun didn't mean Cassie was of the same opinion.

Jake took the phone and turned his back on her. "Eight o'clock will be good, Angelique," he said. "I'll see you at the Pinnacle."

Cassie told herself sternly that there was really no reason to feel let down at the idea that he was going to Denver's finest restaurant with a woman who sounded like the bimbo of the week. So much for his protest that none of Caleb Tanner's beauties had taken him seriously last night.

He put the phone down, and Cassie forced a smile. "Darn," she said. "And here I was just about to ask if you'd like me to throw an extra chop on the grill when I fix my dinner."

"Were you really going to?"

There was an odd soft note in his voice that made

Cassie grit her teeth. Couldn't the man play along with a face-saving joke? Did he have to go for the jugular?

"Don't worry about it," she said. "You've obviously made plans—at the Pinnacle, of all places, and with Angelique…"

"Not exactly. Though she did offer to fix me up with one of her friends."

"Lucky guy." She started to rinse the dishes which had collected in the kitchen sink.

"I told her I was bringing you."

Cassie dropped a mug. "You *what*?"

"Want to go to dinner at the Pinnacle, Cassie?"

"Why? You couldn't get yourself out of a blind date without dragging me into it? What kind of a man-about-town are you, anyway?"

"I thought you'd be pleased. It was your idea."

"*Mine*?"

"Distract the bimbo, you said, and—"

"You want *me* to take her attention off Caleb Tanner—and vice versa? You'd have been better off with the friend—at least they'd have interests in common to talk about. When I mentioned distraction, I was thinking more in terms of importing a famous rock star or an actor or—"

"You're underestimating yourself, Cassie. Here's your chance to meet the playboy millionaire and show him what he's missed by not knowing you."

"I never said it was my life's ambition to make his acquaintance, you know."

"All right, if Caleb Tanner isn't your cup of tea—"

"Not by a long shot. I don't think much of people who can't settle on one thing, whether it's women or jobs or—"

"Careful," Jake chided. "You could be talking about yourself."

Or you, Cassie thought. *And you've said plenty already.*

"And you don't have to approve of the man, just be polite to him. When was the last time you had dinner at the Pinnacle, anyway?"

Cassie had to admit it had been a long time since she'd gone out for an elegant evening. A very long time, in fact.

"Lobster thermidor," Jake said. "Veal parmesan. Steak Diane. Am I making any inroads here?"

And to spend that elegant evening with Jake…

Maybe it's wiser if we don't look too closely into your feelings about that, she told herself. "You'd be a lot better off with Sabrina," she muttered. "Are you certain you don't want her phone number after all?"

CHAPTER SIX

CASSIE brushed her hair till each curl looked like burnished copper, not so much because she was concerned about how it looked—the last thing she wanted to do was leave the impression that she was trying to compete with the bimbo of the week for attention—but to give herself the opportunity for a slightly longer lecture.

"This is not a date," she reminded herself. Jake would never have thought of asking her out for dinner, if he hadn't needed a companion who wouldn't demand his attention tonight—as any friend of Angelique's was likely to—but instead would leave him free to concentrate on his boss.

So Cassie would do exactly that; she'd enjoy her dinner and leave him in peace. Keeping Angelique distracted would be a little more difficult, Cassie expected. Caleb Tanner's bimbo of the week hadn't reached that position by devoting herself to girl talk, that was certain. But surely Jake didn't expect miracles; anything Cassie could accomplish along those lines would be an improvement in his situation.

She gave a last touch up to her mascara and went downstairs. Jake was in the living room, running a hand over the door Buddy had laid out on the sawhorses. "This doesn't look difficult," he said. "I'm surprised—eager as you are to get it fixed—that you haven't got it painted already."

"I'm not the one who'll be doing it. Have you read the instructions?"

"Shouldn't need instructions to paint a flat surface."

"Have you ever painted anything?"

"Not since kindergarten. What's the big deal? You dip the brush and smear." Jake looked around and picked up a screwdriver Buddy had left nearby. "I'm surprised Buddy didn't take the hinges completely off."

"He suggested taping them instead. Jake, this isn't just the average door, and the instructions say to be very careful with sharp instruments, because—"

The screwdriver slipped and left a deep dent in the surface of the door, just down from the top hinge. Jake didn't say a word, just looked at it thoughtfully.

Despite herself, Cassie was impressed. Most of the men she knew would have turned the air blue. "—because the surface is somewhat flexible," she finished.

"That must explain why it was so easy to kick in. You know, maybe instead of replacing this thing, we should hold off and let Roger and Peggy decide whether they want something stronger instead."

"And spend the next week till they get home waiting for the old one to cave in? To say nothing of explaining to Buddy why we're no closer to having the door installed after he went to all the trouble of finding and delivering it? No thanks. You just don't want to get paint on your hands, do you?"

"It's not on my list of hobbies, no." He put the screwdriver down and looked Cassie over. His gaze was calm, and his voice cool. "You look nice."

But what, Cassie mocked herself, had she expected? Stunned admiration and glib compliments? No, she wasn't such a fool.

This is not a date, she reminded herself, and that was why she'd chosen a simple, basic black dress which made no pretense at standing out from the crowd. Of course, her wardrobe didn't boast fancy cocktail gowns, so even if she'd wanted to dazzle him with spangles and sequins, she couldn't have done it.

And even if you owned spangles and sequins, she thought, *he might not be so easily dazzled anyway.*

"I didn't even think to ask if you had something to wear," Jake said. "Or is that one of Peggy's dresses?"

"No, it's mine. You're just lucky that when I picked up the dry cleaning yesterday I wasn't headed across town to my apartment."

"You mean your cardboard box under the bridge has walk-in closets?"

She'd almost forgotten the exchange as he'd been trying to dislodge her that first night, when he'd implied she was actually homeless. "My apartment's only an efficiency, not a lot bigger than a cardboard box—and what I wouldn't give for a walk-in closet." She reached for the casual tweed jacket she'd tossed across the banister when she'd come home from the paint store. "The Pinnacle's all the way downtown. If we're not going to be late, we'd better be going."

He eyed the jacket. "You could borrow a coat from Peggy. She must have something you'd like."

"Peggy has everything, including a black fox cape that would make this dress look like a dust rag—but I wouldn't want to take a chance of losing it. No, thanks. I'll leave this in the coat-check room in the hotel lobby before we go up to the restaurant, and nobody will even see it."

At the entrance to the hotel, Jake turned his keys over to the parking valet and came around the car to help Cassie out. Then he paused on the sidewalk and looked straight up the sheer glass wall of the hotel to a bulge at the top of the tower. "Is that the restaurant up there?"

"How'd you guess?" Cassie asked brightly. "The name, maybe?"

"It doesn't revolve, does it?"

"As a matter of fact, it does. Why? Do you get motion sickness?"

"Not exactly. I just don't trust the gears in these things. The idea of an entire floor resting and rotating on one fixed point makes me nervous."

"Well, you can relax. This one was renovated a few years back."

"How many years?"

"Three or four. They put in all new mechanical systems at the time."

"New stuff, made to modern engineering specifications with modern engineering methods—now that absolutely inspires confidence."

In fact, Cassie thought, Jake sounded anything but convinced. She turned her jacket over to the coat-check clerk and tucked the tiny claim token into her clutch purse. "The elevators are over there."

Jake took her arm as they walked across the lobby, and automatically Cassie dropped into step beside him. His touch was casual, as if he was so much in the habit of strolling with a woman—or, more likely, Cassie thought, a continual series of women—that he didn't even stop to think about it. She wondered what kind of dancer he'd be. A natural, she suspected; it was a shame she would never know for sure.

With an effort she pulled herself back from the brink. How foolish it was to feel regret over something which had never been a possibility.

The elevator lobby was empty, and the indicators showed that most of the cars were high inside the hotel. With an easy touch, Jake turned her to face him.

Yes, she thought. *A natural. A woman would have to try in order not to follow his lead, both in dancing and in other things....*

Cassie took a deep breath in an effort to re-anchor herself to reality. "How can you be in electronics," she asked, "and not be gung-ho about every last technical improvement?"

"Because I've seen how many of them aren't really improvements," Jake said.

She had been vaguely aware of another couple entering the elevator lobby, but she hadn't paid any attention until a man spoke right beside her, in an amused voice she'd heard before. "That's not it, you know," he said. "It's because Jake's not really in electronics. He's in money."

Cassie recognized the face; in the last year Caleb Tanner had graced so many of Denver's home-town publications—even billboards—that he was practically the poster boy for the city. The blonde who was hanging on him, both her hands clasped around his arm as if to hold him as tightly and as close as possible, was less familiar, though she was every bit as photogenic as the millionaire playboy.

Jake introduced them, and Caleb looked down at Cassie with a smile. "So you're the rented wife," he said just as the elevator car signalled its arrival, and suddenly— Cassie had no idea how—he'd freed himself from Angelique's grasp and taken Cassie's arm instead. He guided her into the elevator. "You'll have to tell me all about it. How does the agreement work? By the day? By the week?"

At least he hadn't said *by the hour*, Cassie thought. *Or by the night*. She smothered the desire to flatten him and reminded herself of exactly why she was here. Distracting Caleb from Angelique or Angelique from Caleb—what

was the difference, after all? Not that she was apparently
going to have much choice in the matter; Caleb had apparently decided to make it easy for her.

The elevator delivered them to the Pinnacle, and the
maitre d' broke into a brilliant smile and led them through
the dark little lounge which occupied the stationary center
of the restaurant and out onto the revolving deck, into a
section set off by glass walls to form a private party area.

Two other couples were waiting for them. One of the
women, standing beside a middle-aged man, was as cos-
metically enhanced as Angelique was; she looked startled
to see Cassie on Caleb Tanner's arm instead of her friend.
The other couple were younger, obviously married, and
just as obviously ill-at-ease in their surroundings. The
wife was thin and dark and harried-looking; the husband
was wary.

As Caleb greeted the foursome, Cassie found herself
standing next to Jake, momentarily as alone with him as
if they'd been stranded on a distant planet. "I thought you
told him I was just your answering service," she muttered.

Jake grinned. "Cassie, sweetheart," he said gently,
"surely you aren't innocent enough to think he believed
me?"

But when the initial greetings were finished and Caleb
turned back to Cassie to introduce her, Jake was unac-
countably in the way. "Let me, Caleb," he said.
"Angelique's feeling a little abandoned, I think."

He draped a casual arm around Cassie's shoulders.
"What are you doing?" she muttered. "I thought you
wanted him distracted from her."

"You're doing fine," Jake said under his breath. He
drew her forward to introduce her to the other two couples. It was a Tanner Electronics party from start to finish,
Cassie soon realized, since the middle-aged man who kept

staring at Angelique's friend as if he couldn't quite believe his luck was the production manager. She had a bit more trouble figuring out why the young couple had been included, until Jake said something to the man about how much he'd be missed at Tanner, and expressed the hope that he'd enjoy the challenges to be found in his new job. But even the fact that this was a farewell party didn't keep it from being one of the strangest gatherings Cassie had ever witnessed.

A waitress came to take their drinks order, and soon Cassie was sipping a glass of white wine and watching as Angelique's friend treated the production manager almost like a puppy—tossing him a smile in lieu of a dog biscuit now and then when she remembered him. Angelique was quietly fuming, no doubt because Caleb was paying more attention to Cassie than to her. The young engineer's wife looked as if she'd rather be anywhere else. And Jake hadn't taken his hand off Cassie's shoulder since he'd put it there so possessively, what seemed like an hour ago.

Yet his touch was so casual that Cassie suspected it must look as if he'd forgotten his arm was still draped around her. She couldn't forget, however—and she'd bet her last dollar that he was perfectly aware of what he was doing, too.

You're doing fine, Jake had told her, and it didn't take long for Cassie to see what he'd meant. Caleb—obviously intrigued by what he must think of as a new style of plaything—couldn't keep his attention off Cassie. And that meant, if Jake was sticking to her side like glue as well, he would have the perfect opportunity to observe Caleb, where Angelique couldn't do a thing to interfere.

Cassie could almost find it in her heart to feel sorry for Angelique, who obviously was not going to gracefully accept the fact that her time as bimbo of the week had come and gone. Even her friend knew it, that was obvious. Not only was she paying scant attention to her date, but she was keeping one careful eye on Angelique at the same time she managed to hang adoringly on every word Caleb uttered.

Caleb had one question after another about Rent-a-Wife, and finally Cassie, aggravated at being able to make only fragmentary and—she suspected—misleading explanations, held up her hands to stop the flow of interrogation and gave him the standard spiel, from slogan through philosophy to the list of things Rent-a-Wife didn't do.

When she was finished, silence reigned in the party room for half a minute, more than long enough for Cassie to regret stepping up on her soap box.

Jake drew her a little closer and said mildly, "I love to listen to you reel all that off, Cassie."

"You're very good at presenting the information," Caleb added.

Angelique sniffed. "And I'll bet that's not the only thing she's good at," she said under her breath. "I'm sure that running errands is the very least of her talents."

Her friend giggled.

The engineer's young wife said, "It sounds pretty good to me. I may be at home all the time with two kids, but some days *I'd* like to have a wife."

Cassie sent a grateful smile at her. "I'll give you my card. If we can help you out any time—"

Angelique rolled her eyes. "Are you sure you wouldn't rather be helping *him* instead of *her*?" she said suggestively.

The young woman wouldn't meet Cassie's gaze. "I doubt I could afford you," she said quickly. "Until Eric gets established at a new job, we won't have the money to—"

Cassie saw the engineer's hand close tight on his wife's arm, and the embarrassed color which flooded the young woman's face made her want to cry. She turned away, unwilling to make it worse by watching, and caught a glimpse of Jake. His eyes were narrowed, his attention completely focused on the young woman's face. But there was no trace in his expression of the sympathetic mortification Cassie had felt; he looked as if he'd been mesmerized.

Cassie fumbled in her handbag and held out a business card to the young woman. "Well, take it anyway," she said. "You never know when things will change."

"What's your favorite part of the job?" Caleb asked.

"And how hard did you have to train for it?" Angelique gibed.

Cassie tried to bite her tongue, but she'd had more than she could take of the implications that she was not only too uneducated to be anything more than an errand-runner but too ignorant to know when she was being insulted.

"I've had to learn more for this job than for anything else I've ever done," she said. "And that includes the work it took to get my master's degree in English literature."

Angelique's jaw dropped.

"Not that a specialty like Elizabethan poetry doesn't come in handy now and then," Cassie added sweetly. "For instance, when I'm asked to write love poems for men who can't express themselves to give to women who don't know the difference."

The silence this time was absolute, until Caleb burst into laughter. "That'll teach you, Angelique," he said. "Now let's let the whole subject rest and have dinner, all right?"

Cassie wasn't surprised when Jake maneuvered her to

a seat at the far end of the long table from Angelique. However, when she saw Caleb take the head of the table, next to the bimbo and as far as possible from Jake, she suffered a stab of guilt that her outburst had made it impossible for him to stay in position next to his boss.

She leaned closer to Jake as he sat down beside her. "So much for my people skills," she muttered. "Sorry."

Jake shook his head. "Don't worry about what's done." He opened her menu and handed it to her.

Just as if he was distracting a child, Cassie thought. He might as well have said, *Here's paper and a box of crayons, so draw a picture and don't bother me just now.*

Jake passed a basket of bread-sticks to the engineer and his wife and said easily, "Tell me what you're looking for in a job, Eric."

The young man darted a look at his wife and said in a low voice, "A new challenge."

Cassie stared unseeing at a list which included everything from emu to sweetbreads as she considered the young man's answer. The response sounded rehearsed to her. But then, the question had been no more than a timefiller, asked only because Jake couldn't do what he'd set out to accomplish this evening.

That, of course, was all because of Cassie. Instead of helping, she reminded herself guiltily, she'd managed to get in the way. Her pride had been nicked, and rather than reminding herself why she was there and simply swallowing the insinuation that anyone who'd take on her job must be too stupid to do anything better—a suggestion which had no more validity than the ignorant bimbo who'd voiced it—Cassie had retaliated. She'd reduced herself to Angelique's level, and now Jake was paying the price.

She stared down at the Pinnacle's exotic menu. Suddenly, every item on it sounded like dust and ashes.

Would the evening never end?

Jake had spent his share of time at cocktail parties and receptions, social events where, in fact, business was the only thing everyone held in common. That kind of pseudo-social gathering was the most deadly dull on earth, full of political implication and maneuvering and one-upmanship and generally pretty thin on actual enjoyment.

But this so-called party was the worst he'd ever been subjected to. The conversation limped, the guests apparently had no desire to discover common interests, and he was getting precisely nowhere at finding out why a young engineer who was one of Tanner's best had quit his job without having a new one lined up. Hell, it was only due to pure luck—and Cassie, of course—that he'd found out that much.

And now Cassie wasn't even talking. She'd gone totally silent, until the only noise she made was the rustle of her sleeve as she pushed bits of food around on her plate.

But faint as the sound was, and even though the table was large and the chairs placed at an easy distance, he seemed able to hear nothing but the soft rasp of black velvet against white linen.

She seemed to feel his gaze on her, for she looked up from her plate, her eyes big and a darker blue than he'd seen them before. "I'm really sorry I messed things up for you, Jake."

It was no time for explanations—and what was he supposed to say, anyway? That instead of regretting what she'd said, he'd actually wanted to applaud her for letting the hot air out of Angelique? Or—equally true—that he wished they hadn't sat down, because by doing so he'd lost the excuse to keep an arm around her? That his palm itched with the desire to cup itself around her shoulder and draw her closer?

She'd think he'd lost his mind. Jake wasn't so sure he hadn't.

Or maybe it's just that lilac bath oil of hers going to your head, he told himself. Every time she moved, the scent of spring engulfed him.

Cassie took a long, almost shaky breath, and turned her gaze toward Caleb, who was lounging at the head of the table with Angelique on one side and her friend on the other, both apparently hanging on his every word.

She looked, Jake thought, like a child who'd just spent her last cent on a new toy and then—too late—discovered one she liked better. Her expression was full of regret. Maybe even longing.

Annoyance washed ever him. *I never said it was my life's ambition to make his acquaintance*, she'd said of Caleb Tanner. That had been just a couple of hours ago, yet now she was practically drooling over the man. What on earth did women find so attractive about the playboy millionaire?

"You're hardly his usual style," he said curtly.

For a moment he thought she hadn't heard him, then the dark blue gaze came to rest on his face. "Gee, thanks, Jake. If it wasn't for that reminder, I might never have realized that I came up short."

At least, he thought with an instant's relief, the acid was back in her voice. This was the Cassie he'd come to know. "I meant that as a compliment," he protested. "Anyway, what's the big deal? You had Caleb's full attention earlier, and you didn't seem to want it."

"I didn't—and I still don't. I thought you did. What are you doing here, anyway, Jake? And what did Caleb mean when he said you're not in electronics, you're in money?''

He hadn't expected her to remember that careless comment. ''I'm investigating a request he's made for venture capital funding.''

She looked puzzled. ''He needs more cash?''

''Even millions aren't a lot when you're trying to launch a new product. Besides, it would be foolish to use his own money if investors are available.''

''And that's who you represent? The investors?''

Jake nodded.

''So you're not really working for Caleb at all,'' she mused.

''Not directly, no.''

''No wonder you weren't interested when I suggested finding an apartment. You're not just waiting to see how the job works out, you already know you're not going to be here long enough to need a place to live.''

''I figure my work here will take a few weeks. A month at the top end.''

''And I suppose the job in Florida that kept you from coming to Roger and Peggy's wedding was the same kind of thing?''

''A start-up firm,'' he recalled, ''wanting money to build plastic models. Before that, it was cell phones in San Diego, and before that—''

''And of course that's why you don't bother to put anything perishable in your refrigerator.''

''I'm only in New York between projects. Maybe two months out of the year, total.''

''Home musty home,'' Cassie said. ''But obviously you like it that way. You'd no doubt be bored, staying in one place.''

She sounded almost bitter, he thought. Of course, she

wouldn't be the first woman who'd gotten the idea that he ought to be content to be tied down—with her. But he'd thought Cassie was different. "It's true that I don't deal well with routine, but—"

Cassie shook her head chidingly. "You've been hiding out, you know. Letting people believe you're job-hopping, when you're actually just on temporary assignments."

"You really want me to put my life history on my business card and hand it out to everybody I meet?" He didn't bother to try keeping the incredulity out of his voice.

She bit her lip, and her face turned pink.

"And before you start flinging accusations," Jake went on, "remember that I'm not the only one who hasn't spilled everything I know."

She frowned as if she didn't understand.

"Your master's degree," he reminded. "I remember talking about the reasons you like your job—and I wouldn't have forgotten you saying that you preferred it to tenure in an ivory tower somewhere. That never came up in the discussion."

He thought she looked distinctly uneasy, and he was intrigued. Why should having an advanced degree be such a tender subject? She'd brought it up herself—admittedly only under stress, but she hadn't been forced into the revelation. But the way she was reacting now didn't fit somehow. What was so shameful about admitting that she'd once been at least a budding professor of literature?

He was still thinking about that look of self-conscious apprehension when the party broke up. If she'd had to admit being a porn star, he thought, the reaction would have made a whole lot more sense.

He reclaimed his car from the parking valet and helped Cassie in, and as he pulled out onto Colfax Avenue, she said abruptly, "That business about the master's degree, Jake—I wasn't telling the truth."

He was almost disappointed. The explanation was too easy, too ordinary, to be satisfying. "You don't have one? You were just pulling Angelique's leg?"

"Not exactly." Then she sighed and said, "I just never finished. I quit when I was a few hours short of my degree."

"Why?"

"Lots of reasons." Her voice was short.

"All of which you're going to share, of course."

"I'd hate to bore you. Let's just say I realized at the last minute that it wasn't what I wanted to do—so why waste the time to finish?"

"And let's just say I don't believe that's the whole story. In fact, I don't buy it at all. Does this have anything to do with the guy who treated you so badly?" In the glow of the traffic light which had stopped them, he watched her eyes dilate with apprehension and knew he'd struck pay dirt. "What did he do, Cassie?"

She hesitated, and then she made a helpless little gesture and said, "A whole lot of my master's thesis ended up in an article he wrote for a scholarly journal."

"In other words, he stole your research."

She nodded.

"And that was enough to make you give up your whole career?"

Anger flared in her eyes. "You don't need to make me sound like a quitter, Jake."

"Aren't you?"

"I didn't have a choice. I couldn't prove Stephan had stolen my work—he made very sure of that—and nobody would have taken my word against his."

"Why not?"

For a moment he thought she wasn't going to answer. "Because he was a full professor, specializing in Shakespearean studies."

Jake whistled softly. "And he had to steal insights on Elizabethan poetry from a grad student?"

"See? Who would have believed me?" She bit her lip. "I couldn't stay there, and I couldn't afford to start over somewhere else. My stipend was expiring, my loans were coming due, my fellowship was over. So—"

"So you ended up as a rented wife instead."

"Don't make it sound like some second-class solution, Jake. We all do what we have to, sometimes. Did you dig out what you were after tonight?"

He took a moment to switch gears. "You mean, did I make any judgment about Caleb's character?"

"No, I mean did you get the information you were after from the engineer?"

He stopped for another red light and gave her a long, appraising look. "You figured that out, I see."

"After a certain point in the evening, I didn't have much to do but watch."

"As a matter of fact, you're right. And by the way, thanks, Cassie."

"For what?"

"If it hadn't been for you, his wife wouldn't have confessed that he doesn't have a job to jump to at all."

"And that's important information?"

He debated with himself for a moment before he admitted, "It's very important. It would be one thing if he'd been offered a load of incentives, or if he'd accepted a better position than the one he was giving up. But obviously there's some other reason he was very unhappy with his job. And I need to find out if something's wrong at

Tanner before we sink a whole lot of money into a new product and the campaign to market it.''

He parked the car in front of the townhouse and walked around to open Cassie's door. She didn't move, however, just sat staring at the front door until Jake looked over his shoulder to check out what she'd seen. Nothing was apparently wrong; the door was still in place, the hall lights they'd left on were still blazing, and he could see the shadow of the camera just above the door casing.

"What's wrong at Tanner," Cassie said, "is that Caleb isn't tending to business." She got out of the car and, hands deep in her jacket pockets, hurried toward the house.

Jake caught up with her as she was unlocking the door. "You mean because he's got all the bimbos hanging around. Look, Cassie, I know you didn't hit it off with Angelique, and I know you don't have much of an opinion of Caleb. But I really think the woman is more of a nuisance to everyone else than she is a distraction to him.''

Cassie nodded. "You think he can keep the women in their proper place, and I wouldn't dream of questioning your judgment on that matter.''

Jake wasn't quite sure how to take that.

Cassie pushed the door open. "But you also said the place is controlled chaos—and if it's anything like that party tonight, I'd put my money on the chaos instead of the control.''

"Just because that was a pretty strange party doesn't mean—'' He stopped and thought about what she'd said. *Caleb isn't tending to business*. She was wrong, of course. Caleb lived and breathed that company. But...

"Personally, I've always thought that anytime there's doubt about who's in charge, the boss is not doing his job—and maybe he shouldn't have the position.''

Jake felt his face go blank with surprise.

"But then," Cassie went on hastily, "what do I know about industry and economics and executive management?"

She flitted up the stairs, pausing at the top to lean over the rail. "By the way, Jake…"

Her voice had gone from brisk and businesslike to suddenly sultry, and abruptly Jake's thoughts were light years away from Caleb Tanner, the young engineer and venture capital in general.

One word, he thought. Just one word from her…

"Thanks for dinner," Cassie said. "It was an unforgettable evening." And the guest-room door closed solidly behind her.

Unforgettable indeed, Cassie thought as she turned off the light and lay staring into the darkness. What had gotten into her? Poking her nose into the man's business. Giving him advice on something she knew nothing about. Pouring out her troubled history.

Worst of all, feeling annoyed—even left out—when she'd finally heard the details about his job.

There was no reason, she told herself firmly, that Jake should have confided in her. Not about his job, and not about his life. He didn't have any more reason to give her the details than she'd had to expose all the reasons why she'd quit school. And why she'd done that was beyond her, anyway.

No, he didn't owe explanations to casual acquaintances—and a casual acquaintance was not only all she was, it was all she wanted to be.

So why should it matter that he obviously hadn't considered her important enough to confide in?

CHAPTER SEVEN

CASSIE slept later than usual, and it was thumps and bangs from the direction of the master bath that roused her. Buddy was already hard at work, she deduced. Which meant Jake must have let him in, which meant there was a good chance Jake himself was gone for the day.

Which was just fine with Cassie. She'd lain awake a long time last night, regretting the impulse which had made her share that half-baked, instinctual theory of hers about Caleb Tanner. What had inspired her to give Jake the benefit of her layman's diagnosis of the problems at Tanner Electronics? As if she knew the first thing about the corporation.

Had she gone completely crazy? Apparently Jake had thought so, judging by the look on his face when she'd told him that in her opinion Caleb Tanner wasn't fit for the job he held. She should probably be grateful that he'd maintained his composure instead of straightening her out then and there.

Should she apologize for the way she'd dumped her uninformed opinions on him last night? No, Cassie thought, better to leave it alone. With any luck, perhaps Jake would forget how rash and naive she must have sounded. Questioning Caleb Tanner's suitability to run the company he himself had created from scratch—what kind of fool was she, anyway?

By the time she came downstairs, Buddy had switched to a quieter part of the job, and Cassie hesitated for a moment outside the half-open door of the master suite, wondering if she should check on his progress. Between her unanticipated trip to the paint store and Caleb Tanner's party, she hadn't had a chance to inspect his work at all yesterday.

I'll do it later, she thought. She just didn't feel up to dealing with Buddy—or anybody else—right now.

As she came downstairs, however, she was startled by the scent of paint drifting from the living room, where Jake was leaning over the new door, brush in hand.

Cassie tried not to notice the way his well-worn jeans clung just right to his narrow hips, or the way his smile lit his eyes as he looked up over the paint-laden brush and said, "The coffee should be done by now."

Cassie could not only smell it, her heart was tripping as if she'd already consumed the whole pot of caffeine.

Her reaction had nothing to do with his smile, she told herself, except for the reassurance it provided that he wasn't going to make a big deal out of her ill-advised comments last night. And, she thought, if he was going to ignore that gaffe, she'd be happy to play along. "I bet you're going to say you made it just for me."

"Of course not," he admitted, and then grinned. "I was actually thinking of Buddy."

"Sure, you were. Thanks for letting him in, Jake. You didn't have to stick around to keep an eye on him, though. You could have gotten me up."

Jake grinned. "I'll remember that invitation."

Cassie felt her cheeks flame. "I didn't mean it that way."

"Just my luck," he said mournfully.

Before she could get in any deeper, Cassie went to the kitchen, filled two cups and carried them back to the living room. If she had any sense, she thought, she'd hand

Jake his, take the other cup upstairs to Buddy and retreat to the kitchen to make her list for the day.

Instead, she leaned against the arched doorway between living room and foyer and watched as Jake painted with slow, patient, sensual strokes, creating a seamless surface. "That's looking good. Maybe you're a handyman just waiting to be discovered, after all."

Jake shook his head. "Don't bet any money on it. I took your advice and read the directions."

"And you're actually admitting it?" Cassie gave an admiring whistle.

He made a face at her. "This is turning out darker than the original door, though."

"The guy who mixed the paint promised that it's a match. Paint always lightens as it dries."

"I hope he's right. I'd hate to get it all painted and have to start over again."

"You sound as anxious as I am to get it installed."

"I'd like to have it all ready, in case Buddy finds somebody to do the work." He glanced at his watch and dipped the brush again.

"What's the hurry? If he didn't say anything when he came in this morning, he's not likely to find someone before lunch."

"Painting just takes more time than I thought it would."

"Well, you're not exactly subject to a time clock, and surely after last night, Caleb can't object to you taking a couple of hours for some personal business."

"I doubt it. But he's coming by a little later."

"Here?" Cassie knew she sounded horrified. "Why?"

"Because we need some uninterrupted time. At the office, if it isn't bimbos interfering, it's engineers waiting in line for him to look at their technical difficulties. And

he can't go out in public without tripping over women."
Jake braced one hand against the unpainted portion of the
door in order to reach the farthest corner.

It looked, Cassie thought, as if he was still favoring the
shoulder he'd banged up the night he'd burst through the
door. Well, perhaps that lingering pain would remind him
to think first next time—and save him a lot of trouble in
the long run.

Still, there were ways to help the situation. "Buddy
thought when he set those sawhorses up that I'd be the
one doing the painting," she said. "They could be raised
higher, to make it easier for you."

Jake shrugged. "I'm almost done with this side." He
pulled the brush along the edge of the door and said, without looking at her, "I wonder if you'd do me a favor,
Cassie?"

"You're out of olives?"

"Not yet. I want you to get in touch with that young
woman from last night, and see if you can find out any
more about why her husband quit his job."

He actually wanted her help? Trusted her judgment?
Cassie's heart was racing, and it took effort to keep her
voice level. "You mean spy," she said thoughtfully.

Jake let the newly dipped brush dangle over the door.
"Let me guess. You're going to tell me Rent-a-Wife is
too ethical to do industrial espionage."

"I don't think we've ever been asked to before,"
Cassie mused. "This might mark the start of a whole new
line of business—and we could certainly stand the expan-
sion. Sure, I'll do it."

"Thanks, Cassie." It was a different smile this time,
slower and more tender, and altogether more dangerous
to her equilibrium.

She forced herself to look away. "You're dripping paint all over," she pointed out unsteadily.

Jake smoothed out the extra drops. "Can you do it today? The sooner I have hard information…"

The sooner he could make his decisions and the sooner he could move on. He didn't have to say it; the end of the sentence was apparent.

Cassie's mood plummeted. He hadn't asked for her help because he put great stock in her opinions; he'd done it simply because she was available, because she could do the job. She was a means to an end—nothing more.

The reminder shouldn't have come as a shock to Cassie, but nevertheless it settled like a lump in her throat.

He was looking at her quizzically.

"Sure," Cassie managed to say. "I'll stop by with a Rent-a-Wife pamphlet. She doesn't have to know we don't usually deliver them in person."

"Great. I'll get the address as soon as I go into the office." Jake ran the brush once more down the edge of the door and stood back to admire his handiwork. "I think that's all the damage I can do here, till this dries enough to do the other side." He fitted the lid back on the paint and went off to wash out his brush.

Cassie didn't move from the doorway. She leaned her head against the wall, closed her eyes, and gave herself a lecture.

It's crazy for you to be upset, she told herself. Of course Jake was going to use any available avenue to find out what he needed to know; that was, after all, his job. Why should she expect to be treated any differently?

At least he was honest about it, she noted. He'd asked for what he wanted straight out. He could have manipulated her….

He could have *tried*, she corrected.

But none of that answered the original question—why was she upset? Or did she even want to think about that?

She heard Buddy's footsteps on the stairway, but ostrich-like, she stayed stubbornly in place. If she pretended not to hear him, perhaps he'd just go on about his business and leave her alone.

Buddy paused at the foot of the stairs, and his step sounded uncertain as he crossed the foyer toward her. "Ma'am?"

Couldn't the man take a hint? *Stupid question*, Cassie told herself. She swallowed her annoyance and opened her eyes.

Buddy's new haircut still gave her a jolt each time she saw him; relieved of the weight of his ponytail, the hair on top of his head managed to stand up almost straight, though it obviously wasn't intended to do so. She concentrated on his earnest face instead, and the honest concern she saw there made her feel ashamed of her short temper. It wasn't his fault she was annoyed at Jake, after all. "What is it, Buddy?"

"Are you all right, ma'am?"

"Never been better." Cassie tried, without success, to keep the irony out of her voice. "What can I do for you?"

Buddy rocked on his heels and shifted his toothpick from one corner of his mouth to the other. "It's the plumbing, you see."

Cassie wanted to swear, but she knew Buddy was incapable of deliberate obscurity. "Could you be a little more specific?"

"I've hooked the new lines into the old ones, but I keep getting leaks. Not at the new joints, I mean—they're in the old pipes. Every time I patch one up, another one springs open. There's brittle pipe everywhere up there. I just can't guarantee that the system won't pop a seam somewhere and make like a fountain all through the house.''

"So you're saying more of the plumbing needs to be replaced than you expected? It seems to me that should have been anticipated in your original bid, Buddy.''

"Maybe so, ma'am, but these things happen. It looked just fine till I cut into it. This townhouse is twenty years old, at least, and the plumbing was a cut-rate job from the first. It would really be better to put in new pipes from top to bottom. It would make the water pressure a lot stronger, too—it'd fill that tub up in half the time.''

Cassie wasted a few moments imagining the scene if Peggy came home to find that her whirlpool tub was in place as promised but all the rest of the plumbing in the townhouse was gone.

"I'll pass the information along," she said. "But for now you'll just have to do the best you can to patch the leaks, because a complete replumbing is not the kind of work I can authorize without consulting—''

She broke off as Buddy gritted his teeth. Cassie actually heard them grind together, and she watched in fascination as a little muscle twitched in his jaw.

"He doesn't think you can decide anything, does he?'' Buddy's voice had lost all trace of his trademark slow drawl. "He doesn't think you have a mind—that blankety-blank husband of yours.''

Cassie couldn't believe her ears. Had he really just said *blankety-blank*? Then she realized what he'd meant, and she said hastily, "Are you talking about Jake? He isn't my husband.''

Buddy's frown grew even more ominous. "To my way of thinking, that only makes it worse. He tries to scare you, doesn't he? And when you make a fuss—''

"If you're talking about the fact that he broke in the door, that was a misunderstanding."

"Don't bother to make excuses for him, ma'am. I took his measure long ago."

Cassie rubbed her temples and tried again. "Buddy, you've got this all wrong."

"And then to know that he won't even marry you," Buddy said fiercely. "I can't stand it. I won't stand it."

Fancy that, Cassie thought. *A plumber who's addicted to soap operas!*

But the fragments of wry humor she'd found in the situation fled as Buddy's hands closed on her shoulders and pulled her toward him. He seized her chin in one big, rough hand and forced her face up.

"Jake," she said, but her throat was so tight the word was little more than a hoarse whisper.

"I've tried to mind my own business," Buddy announced. "I don't hold with making trouble between husband and wife. But if you're not married to him…if you're free, then everything's different."

Cassie ducked her head, and his kiss landed awkwardly on the side of her face.

"Don't fight me," he said. "I would never hurt you. Let me show you…" His mouth was a bare inch away from Cassie's.

From just behind Buddy, Jake said coolly, "This is very instructional, Buddy, but I suspect Cassie would rather postpone any further lessons—indefinitely." His hand closed ruthlessly on Buddy's shoulder and pulled him away.

Freed, Cassie collapsed against the banister, breathing hard.

"She's not your property," Buddy growled. "If you won't marry her, you've got nothing to say about what she does. So just back off.'' He sidestepped and loosed a fist toward Jake's midsection.

Jake shoved him out of range, and Buddy staggered heavily back, his shoulders hitting squarely against the center of the already-weakened front door.

Cassie stood frozen in disbelief as, almost in slow motion, the door gave a tortured groan and split from top to bottom. The two halves bent outward, a position they'd never been intended to take, and through the crack between them she could see across the parking lot to the little park at the center of the development. A stray shaft of sunlight poked through the gap, highlighting the dust motes and infinitesimal white fibers which floated in the air. A few of them landed on Buddy's head as he sat half-stunned against the broken door.

Jake took three steps toward him and offered a hand up, but Buddy shook his head fiercely and struggled to his feet on his own. ''I wouldn't take your hand if my life depended on it,'' he spat.

Jake shook his head a little, as if he couldn't believe what he was hearing. ''After the scene you just created, you have some gall to accuse *me* of misbehaving.''

Cassie said hastily, ''I think it would be better if everybody cooled off for a while. If you two would just go to neutral corners for a bit and think it over, I'm sure you'll realize—''

Buddy stared at her. ''You don't want to be rescued, do you? You like having him treat you like this. All right, I get the message. I'll pick up my tools another time.'' He dusted off his jeans, kicked one section of the door out of his way, and was gone. A few seconds later the roar of a pickup truck announced his departure.

The ensuing silence in the foyer pressed painfully against Cassie's eardrums. She sat down on the lowest step. "Gee, thanks, Jake," she said, without bothering to moderate the sarcasm she felt.

"Wait a minute," Jake protested. "If you didn't want my help, why did you yell?"

"I didn't."

"You certainly did." Jake paused. "Well, maybe it was more of a strangled whisper than an actual yell, but you certainly were calling my name."

"And you came flying to the rescue, didn't you—in a manner of speaking—so now we're not only short a door, we're short a plumber."

"What—Oh, you mean that bit about picking up his tools."

"What else could he have meant? He's off the job. I'm just surprised he didn't give you the standard line about not working for you if you were the last employer on the face of the earth. I think it was the only cliché he left out, but maybe he's saving that one for when he gathers up his stuff. Nevertheless—"

"What did he mean by saying you don't want to be rescued?"

"He thinks I'm defending you despite the fact that you've been abusing me."

"That's absurd."

"Is it? You told him you kicked the door in because I locked you out. That isn't exactly the mark of a calm, even temperament, Jake. What would you expect him to think?"

"So, because I'm supposed to have been acting like a cave man, he takes that as permission to follow suit?"

"He thought he was doing me a favor."

"Now you're defending him."

"I'm just explaining why it wasn't necessary for you to hit him."

"I didn't hit him. All I did was pull him away from you."

"You shoved him."

"He was trying to slug me. And one more thing, Cassie. Don't forget if I hadn't been here to stop him, he would have—"

"—*not* carried on like a soap star," Cassie cut in. "Because he'd have had no reason to be obsessed."

"Sweetheart, if you think it's me that Buddy's obsessing about, you have a very naive view of the world—and of the men in it."

She was uneasily aware that she hadn't quite explained her leap in logic, and that she had no intention of trying to do so. But the fact was, if Jake had gone to work that morning instead of painting the door, she wouldn't have been standing in the foyer trying to talk herself out of being annoyed with him and Buddy would have had no reason to react so strongly. It would have been just another day around the townhouse.

"What had you said to him, anyway?" Jake asked suspiciously. "Did you put the maggot in his brain about me marrying you?"

Cassie had hoped he'd missed that little twist, but it was just her luck that he hadn't. Of course, she reflected, a man like Jake wouldn't be likely to overlook a mention of marriage in any context which might affect him personally. Alertness on the subject must be the first line of defense for a man who was allergic to the whole idea of settling down.

But the idea that he was trying to put the blame on *her* for Buddy's misunderstanding sent her blood pressure soaring.

"Oh, that," she said sweetly. "The only thing I said to him about marriage was that I've begged and begged you to make an honest woman of me, but any time I bring up the subject you refuse even to consider it, and then you beat me even harder. I don't understand why he should get so upset at you over that, but—''

Jake's voice was pleasantly matter-of-fact. ''Keep that up, Cassie, and beating will be too good for you.''

Cassie rolled her eyes. ''Jake, you idiot. Buddy seems to be a little confused about who's who. Now that I think about it, I don't recall ever explaining the whole setup to him—that I'm just the house-sitter and you're only a guest.''

Jake frowned. ''He's got us mixed up with Peggy and Roger?''

''It makes sense, doesn't it? We're here, in their house. Unless you explained about their camping trip and all…?''

Jake shook his head. ''The only subject I've discussed with Buddy is the door.''

''Well, then it's no wonder he was confused. He was expecting us to behave like a happily married couple, and instead he landed in the middle of what must look like a melodrama.''

''I don't care how confused he was, it's no excuse for what he did.''

''Well, if you're expecting me to thank you for interfering, Jake, I'm afraid you're in for a wait. If you think I can't take care of myself—''

''Right,'' Jake jeered. ''You were doing such a good job of it when I walked in. Damn, it makes me wish I hadn't taken a hand in it. I'd have enjoyed seeing you break out your martial arts black belt and paste Buddy to the floor.''

Cassie bit her lip.

His voice gentled. "At least admit it, Cassie. You were in way over your head."

She didn't look him in the eye, but she thought she heard a hint of indulgence in his voice, and it made her say stubbornly, "I can take care of myself."

Jake shook his head almost sadly and turned away, and Cassie released a tiny breath of relief.

She must have closed her eyes for an instant, for she didn't see his feint become an attack. She only knew that an instant later she was in his arms, the entire length of her body pressed hard against his, only her toes touching the floor, completely helpless and unable to move.

Buddy's hold had been awkwardly determined. Jake's was like being wrapped in velvet cord—but the velvet concealed steel cable. It wouldn't leave a mark, but it was impossible to escape. Buddy had been scary; Jake was terrifying.

"Don't." Her voice was no more than a feeble breath. "Let me go, Jake."

"Now's your chance to demonstrate how you take care of yourself, Cassie. How are you going to stop me from doing anything I please?" He lowered his head until his lips brushed hers as he whispered, "Show me how you do it. Protect yourself."

She twisted in his arms, but she couldn't get leverage enough to escape. If she could only get her feet firmly on the floor...

His mouth came down on hers, firm and demanding. Cassie's head spun, and she forgot all about her feet. What was the point in thinking about a body part she couldn't even feel any more—especially when there were so many others shrieking with sensation?

She knew she had to free herself from that kiss without an instant's delay, though not because it was unpleasant or harsh or demeaning or hurtful. Quite the contrary, in fact. But if she didn't bring this embrace to a screeching halt soon, Cassie knew she was going to be nothing more than a quivering mass of sensation, unable to move or think or act.

With her last logical thought, she deliberately went limp in his arms. If Jake thought she'd capitulated, he'd have nothing left to prove, and even if he didn't release her immediately, he'd be off his guard and she could strike whenever she chose. Better yet, if she could make him think she'd actually fainted, he'd surely let her go— for there couldn't be any challenge in kissing an unconscious woman. And that was the whole point, wasn't it— the challenge? He was simply proving that he was strong enough to do whatever he liked.

It wasn't a bad plan, and with someone else it would probably even have worked. But she'd underestimated Jake. As Cassie's eyes closed and her body slackened in his arms, he drew her closer yet, taking every ounce of her weight against his own strength. Abruptly, his kisses gentled.

If he'd continued to demand, if he'd tried to force her, she could have gathered her strength and fought him. Instead, every touch and every kiss coaxed her to respond, and there wasn't enough will power in the world to keep Cassie safe from the seductive taste of him.

"There's a nice couch right around the corner," he said against her lips.

Cassie knew something was wrong with that scenario, but it took her hazy brain nearly half a minute to remember what it was. "The door's standing wide open."

"Do you think that's going to stop me?" His voice was a tender growl against her throat. Cassie let her head fall back against his shoulder as he guided her into the living room and down onto the nearest chair. She sank into its depths and waited for him to join her. But he didn't.

She managed to open her eyes, though her vision swam as she looked up at him. "What's wrong, Jake?"

"As you pointed out, the door's standing wide open," he said. "Not that the idea of having an audience seemed to bother you much."

Infuriated, Cassie leaped up from the chair, and, as she spun round to face him, her thigh bumped the edge of the newly painted door. Teal-blue paint seemed to leap gleefully onto her tweed slacks. She swore and brushed ineffectually at the stain, seething at the damage to a brand-new outfit but also, in a convoluted way, glad to have the excuse not to look at Jake—and the excuse to avoid inspecting the possible truth of what he'd said.

"And we've both discovered that your method of defending yourself rests entirely on somebody else's self-control." Jake's voice had a ragged edge, as if he was having trouble getting his breath. "But we've also found out something else, Cassie. It wasn't what I set out to prove, but there's no denying it's real. You want me as badly as I want you."

"That's not true. You attacked me."

"No. I kissed you. And you kissed me back. You can't run away from this, Cassie. We have some things to work out."

She shook her head. Carefully, she tried to sidestep him, but he moved ever so slightly and braced his hands against the wall above her shoulders, pinning her into place.

"We have some things to work out," he repeated. "And don't give me any nonsense about how your buddy the professor disillusioned you too much ever to have anything to do with a man, because I'm not like him, and I'm not taking on his baggage. I won't lie to you, Cassie.''

"I never said you were like him.''

"Good," he whispered. "I'm glad to have that much straight." He bent his head to kiss her once again.

Only his mouth was touching her, and yet Cassie was as firmly trapped as if he'd wrapped her in a net. She could barely breathe; every function of her body seemed to slow as her focus narrowed to the caress of his lips against hers.

Her little guttural growl brought a sparkle to Jake's eyes. "My sentiments exactly," he said. "So what are we going to do about it?''

Cassie's voice was shaky. "We're not going to have an affair, that's sure.''

Jake's mouth drifted across the line of her jaw to nibble at her earlobe. "We already *are* having an affair. We just haven't gotten as far as the bedroom yet.''

She ducked her head and turned away, but—undeterred—Jake shifted his attention to her temple.

"I see." Cassie tried to keep her voice light. "Well, that must explain why I don't recall sleeping with you. I thought surely it couldn't have just slipped my mind, but—''

"Oh, you'll remember it all right," Jake said gruffly. "I'll guarantee it." The tip of his tongue teased her tiny crystal earring. She could hear the uneven edge of desire in his breathing, and it made her ears buzz.

Jake drew back with a long sigh. "There's Caleb now.''

Cassie twisted around, expecting to see an interested face peering through the gap in the door.

"In the parking lot," Jake said. "That unholy noise is his motorcycle.''

The buzzing in Cassie's ears resolved itself into the roar of a powerful engine. "I'm going," she said hastily.

"Running away?"

"Not at all," Cassie said tartly. "It's just that I don't have much time to get water on this paint smear or it'll be a permanent stain."

"Well, leaving isn't a bad choice," Jake observed. "You look a little ruffled. I'll see you later—unless you'd like me to tell Caleb I need a couple more hours this morning for...what did you call it? Oh, I remember. Personal business." His voice, low and silky, was as much a caress as his kisses had been. "*Very* personal business."

"Don't bother on my account."

"Very well. Have fun...anticipating."

She didn't look at him. "Don't bet on it, Jake. I have far too much to do today to think about you."

"You'll find time."

Cassie swallowed hard and wished she could be as certain of herself as Jake sounded.

CHAPTER EIGHT

CASSIE went straight into the bathroom at the top of the stairs, and Jake stood in the foyer, his eyes half shut, trying to visualize the picture hidden behind the closed door.

The task wasn't at all difficult, he found. The paint smear had been on the back of her leg, so she couldn't possibly deal with it unless she took off her slacks. She must be standing there in her silky blouse and not much else....

Funny, he thought, that an imaginary image of Cassie half dressed could be more erotic than any explicit photograph he'd ever seen. But then photos didn't leave behind the scent of lilacs and the lingering warmth of clinging arms and responsive lips.

We're not going to have an affair, she'd said.

Jake grinned. It would be interesting to see how long her resolve lasted—especially since she'd sounded a little shaky even as she'd made that grandstand statement.

Caleb's face appeared in the gaping hole which was all that remained of the front entrance. "I'd ring the bell," he said mildly, "but it seems redundant when you're obviously maintaining an open-door policy."

"You're the first to try it out. Come on in."

Caleb stepped carefully through the debris. "You know, it's disappointing to realize that you haven't found the solution after all."

Jake was inspecting the remains of the door, wondering how best to secure the pieces. The only answer he could

132

see at the moment was to board the whole thing up till he could finish painting the new door and find someone to install it. "The solution to what?"

"To the age-old problem of the discontented woman." Caleb shook his head sadly. "If a wife you've only rented is the cause of something like this, just think of the damage she could have accomplished if you'd actually married her."

Jake shot a look at him. Caleb Tanner was the last man on earth he'd expect to have the subject of marriage on the brain—but of course it wasn't Caleb's own life he was discussing, so perhaps that accounted for the anomaly.

"A woman threw a drink at me once," Caleb mused. "Hit me smack in the nose. It was one of those sickly-sweet ice cream concoctions, too—of course she couldn't toss a nice Scotch and soda. But I've never had one break down a door to get at me. Or away from me, either. Come to think of it, was she coming or going when this happened?"

"Neither," Jake said shortly. Caleb's nonchalant attitude was rubbing him the wrong way, though he supposed it was unfair of him to be annoyed that Caleb seemed to see the whole thing as a joke. After all, Caleb hadn't seen Cassie's pale, frightened face. Caleb hadn't seen Buddy looming over her, threatening her....

All his life, Jake had heard people describe sudden anger as seeing red, but he'd always thought it was just a figure of speech. And it was true, he admitted, that he hadn't exactly seen *red*; it had been a whole lot more than that. His entire field of vision had not only turned crimson, but it had crackled with flames for a few seconds, precisely as long as it had taken to pull the bully away from her. Jake had never had a more satisfying moment in his life than the instant when Buddy had staggered back and smashed into the door.

Of course, he was going to be paying for that satisfaction for a while longer, Jake admitted. It would have been a whole lot smarter to toss him against the wall instead of the door. Cassie said they were going to have to replace the wallpaper anyway because it was torn, so a few blood-stains more or less wouldn't matter much. That way they'd still have had at least the semblance of a front door.

But what was done couldn't be changed now.

He wondered if the piece of plywood Buddy had left upstairs as a shelf to hold his tools was big enough to seal up the opening. It would be fitting, somehow, to use the man's own property to fix the damage he'd done.

Jake was still fitting the larger chunks of the door back into place, with Caleb's supervision, when Cassie came out of the bathroom and down the steps. From the closet just inside the foyer she took a leather handbag as big as a mail pouch.

Deliberately, Jake didn't move out of her path. "I see you got rid of the paint stain."

She fussed with the pouch's strap, settling it into place on her shoulder, and didn't look at him. "It's amazing what you can do with cool water, hand soap and a hair dryer. Hello, Caleb," she said politely. "Thanks again for the party last night. I'll see you later, Jake."

He put out a hand to stop her. "You might want to hunt up a key to the French doors before you go, because this one's going to be out of commission for a while."

Her gaze came up to meet his. "I don't even know where to look. Do you have to board it up?"

He didn't say a word, just touched the door with the tip of his index finger. A piece fell out.

"All right," Cassie said. "I get the point—it was a

stupid question. But I really don't know where to find a key. You'd better call a locksmith.''

"I figured you'd know a good one. Just put it on my bill.''

"At this rate, your bill is going to outlive you.'' She ducked through the still-open hole. The strap of her bag caught on a sharp edge and pulled her up short.

Jake untangled the strap, but he didn't immediately let go of it. "See you later, Cassie,'' he said gently.

The words were innocuous, but it was clear to Jake that she knew exactly what he meant, for she swallowed almost convulsively. His fingertips itched to touch the fluttery pulse at the base of her throat. She tugged the strap from his grip and hurried away.

Caleb coughed. "Better watch your step, Abbott.''

Since he clearly wasn't asking a question, Jake didn't even consider answering. "Let's grab a cup of coffee and talk.''

In the kitchen, Caleb straddled a chair and cradled his mug in one big hand. "Go ahead and hit me with it.''

Jake paused in the midst of pouring his own coffee. "Maybe you should tell me why you're expecting bad news.''

"Because if it was good, you could have given it to me in my office.''

"Not necessarily. There would still be details to work out, and there are too many distractions around the office. But as a matter of fact, I haven't yet made up my mind. There are a lot of things still to think through.''

"Tell me what else you need in order to make your decision, and I'll make sure you get it.'' Caleb set down his cup and shifted in his chair. "Otherwise, I'm going back to the office where I can tinker with spring-powered motors, because doing something would be a whole lot more fun than sitting around watching you think.''

Jake raised his eyebrows. "I thought you turned that idea over to the research and development people."

"You know the old saying. If you want something done right, do it yourself."

A voice echoed through Jake's head. A feminine voice. What was it Cassie had said last night? *Caleb's mind isn't on his business*...something like that.

It was an interesting observation—though she hadn't been precisely correct, of course. If anything, Jake told himself thoughtfully, Caleb's mind was too squarely fixed on his business. Every last iota of his business.

Maybe Cassie had hit on something after all. What else had she been talking about? If the boss wasn't clearly in charge, maybe someone else should be...something like that.

"Humor me," Jake said, "and answer a couple of questions."

Caleb shrugged and settled back into his chair.

"What do you miss most about the early days? What did you like best about Tanner Electronics when you first started it?"

Caleb frowned into his coffee cup for a full minute. "Figuring out answers," he said finally. "That's what I liked best. Taking a technological problem and finding a way to solve it. Being part of the team instead of just looking over their results weeks after the fact when the paperwork lets up for a minute and I have time."

"You liked the practical engineering, in other words."

"That *is* how the company started."

"I know." Jake leaned back, as relaxed as if the question he was about to ask was only a casual, careless one. "I don't suppose you've ever thought of going back to

that. Being an engineer again instead of the head hon-
cho.''

"You mean sell out?''

"No.'' Jake paused. "Well, maybe—though I hadn't
considered that possibility. I was thinking about simply
bringing someone in to fill that office. If you were to hire
an experienced executive officer, somebody with the administrative gifts and talents Tanner needs right now—''

"All the attributes I don't have, you mean.''

"You could do anything you set your mind to, Caleb,
so don't make excuses. The question is whether you want
to, when you could hire an executive type to do all the
work you hate.''

"It would mean giving up control.''

"Day-to-day command, yes. But you could promote
yourself to chairman of the board.''

"You're telling me I'm not fit to run my own company.''

"No. I'm saying that it's perfectly possible for a guy
to be an ingenious entrepreneur but...'' He paused, considering the best way to phrase the thought.

"A lousy manager,'' Caleb said.

Well put, Jake thought. Nobody would ever accuse
Caleb Tanner of being mealy-mouthed. "The fact is, not
everybody can do everything well. It takes one kind of
thinking to start a company, but a completely different
kind to nurture it to maturity.''

"And you don't think I have the right stuff.''

"Businesses seldom move smoothly from garage to executive suite, especially when the boss is as new at the
game as the company is. Your vision would still be important, Caleb. You'd make the policy for a CEO to carry
out, but every day you could be sitting at your workbench
tinkering instead of hassling with the details.''

There was no answer, but Jake hadn't really expected one—and he wasn't about to press. He'd learned, in his work, to give a man time to think. The odds were, if he wasn't pressed, he'd eventually come around.

The philosophy worked in other arenas, too, of course. Take Cassie, for instance.

She'd come around, too. All he had to do was be patient.

And hope that he didn't run out of time.

It took Cassie twice as long as normal to get through her list of errands; she kept missing the obvious and having to retrace her steps, and she was running late when she pulled up in front of the house where she was to meet Paige and Sabrina and the client who wanted their help in sorting out everything left in her mother's home. There were three cars already filling the driveway—the client's Volvo, Sabrina's convertible, and Paige's minivan—and Cassie took a spot on the street and hurried toward the house.

Paige met her at the front door. "Cassie, what's the matter with you? You phoned yesterday, hung up on me and didn't call back till this morning. You set up this meeting yourself just two hours ago, and now you're late for it. What's wrong?"

From behind Paige, Sabrina cast a sharp look at Cassie and said casually, "Give her a break, Paige. It's probably just a touch of spring fever."

"This is October," Paige said acidly.

Sabrina grinned. "Then it's no wonder she's confused."

Paige rolled her eyes, but her face gentled and she gave Cassie an apologetic look. "The truth is, I was starting to get worried. This isn't like you."

"Sorry, Paige. I was exchanging Mrs. Carlson's books at the library, and finding something she hasn't already read is becoming a bigger challenge by the week." Cassie soothed her conscience; the excuse was true, as far as it went.

As they walked through the house, Sabrina dropped into step beside Cassie. "I will now accept your thanks for distracting Paige so she didn't notice your frazzled state," she murmured. "So what's really on your mind?"

"You mean besides the idea that we should enroll ourselves in a self-defense class?"

Sabrina's eyebrows arched. "What brought that up? Was Ben Orcutt on your client list this morning along with Mrs. Carlson?"

Cassie shook her head, already regretting the comment.

By the time they'd toured the entire house and noted all the client's wishes, Cassie had gotten her balance back. With a little time and distance, she could see the situation much more clearly, and she was almost amused at how she'd over- reacted this morning.

All that had happened, really, was a kiss that had gotten a bit out of hand. The worst thing she could do was go around acting as if something significant had occurred between her and Jake, when in fact it hadn't. The best way to handle the situation was to be casual and act exactly as if nothing had happened at all.

Jake might even welcome that approach, she thought. He was probably going to be a little nervous himself, wondering if Cassie was going to interpret events in a more serious light than he'd intended. It might take a little time to convince him that she was no more interested in any sort of relationship than he was in a permanent one— but surely they could put themselves back on a casual footing.

And that would take care of the problem. Wouldn't it?

As they left the client's house, Cassie stopped Paige. "I'm going to be bidding a wallpaper job before long. Do you have a formula for that?"

"Of course she does," Sabrina said under her breath. "Paige has a formula for everything."

Paige unlocked her minivan and put her briefcase inside. "Who's wallpapering?"

"It's Peggy's foyer."

"I thought she liked that paper. And it's almost brand-new, too—I just put it up when they moved in."

Cassie didn't look at her. "There's a tear. Well, it's more of a nick, really. But it's right inside the front door, almost at eye level, so it can't be ignored."

"And this is the same door..." Sabrina pursed her lips as if to release a long, interested whistle.

Cassie elbowed her, and she subsided.

Paige opened her mouth as if to demand an explanation, then seemed to think better of it. "If it's just a patch job, there might be enough paper left to fix it. Check the top shelf in the linen closet—I think that's where we put the scraps." She nodded at the box Cassie was carrying. "If you're not excited by the prospect of sorting out all those insurance papers..."

"How'd you guess?"

Paige smiled. "I'm psychic. Let me take them."

Cassie handed over the box without hesitation. "I'll swap you any job you like—and I mean *anything*. I got one look at this mess and that was enough to discourage me."

Paige shook her head. "I won't blackmail you. Actually, I'm looking for jobs I can do at home right now."

"Is your mother worse?" Cassie asked.

"I don't think so. But she gets a little anxious these days when I'm gone for hours at a time, so I'm going to try to work at home more." Paige set the box into the back of the minivan. "I'll see you two later." In another minute, the minivan was pulling away.

Sabrina dug into her handbag for her car keys. "Sometimes I'd like to give Paige a good shake."

Cassie, already on her way to her car, stopped abruptly. "Over Eileen?"

"Of course. Eileen gets anxious, so Paige rearranges her life to accommodate her. This isn't the first time, and it won't be the last."

Cassie said wistfully, "At least Paige still has her mother. Sometimes I'd give anything to be able to rearrange my life to accommodate mine."

"Ouch," Sabrina said. "I'm sorry, honey."

Cassie smiled. "Don't beat yourself up. It's okay."

"No, it's not. Just hit me over the head with the nearest rock, will you?"

"Sabrina, it's been twelve years since Mom died."

"That's no excuse for me being clumsy. How I could have let it slip my mind..."

"Why should you remember? You never even knew her."

"Well, you've never met my mother either, but that's a little different situation."

Cassie tried to smile. "In a way, your problem is even sadder. I could at least visit my mother's grave, if it wasn't so far away."

"Where's she buried?"

"Indiana."

"Why?" Sabrina sounded horrified.

"Because that's where we were living at the time," Cassie said matter-of-factly. "That was the year my father was going to make it big by turning reproductions of classic cars into lawn furniture.''

"And this man is still walking around loose?"

Cassie looked at her in mock chagrin. "You mean you wouldn't have invested in his business?"

"Only if I'd gotten stuck with a few counterfeit bills. Sorry, Cassie. I should obviously keep my opinions to myself—since I'm hardly a whiz at family relationships.''

Cassie wondered if the note of sadness she thought she heard in Sabrina's voice was only her own imagination. Sabrina had certainly never expressed any regret over being disowned by her parents, or over the choices she'd made which had led to that falling-out. Still, it had been a couple of years now since Sabrina had had any contact with them. Was she feeling the loss?

But Cassie knew better than to ask. Sabrina would only make a joke and turn the question aside.

When Cassie got back to the townhouse, the parking spot directly in front was conveniently empty. Only when she started up the sidewalk did she realize that the front entrance was no longer a hole; it had been blocked up with a chunk of plywood which was securely bolted to the remains of the door.

And only then did Cassie remember that she'd intended to stop at the locksmith's shop.

She retreated to her car, looked up the locksmith's number in her voluminous address book, and called from her cell phone to schedule an appointment for the next day. Then she gathered up her possessions, ready to walk all the way around the townhouse complex and try to find Roger and Peggy's garden beyond one of twenty-five identical fences and gates. And then, no doubt, she'd find herself sitting on the patio because the French doors would be locked and Jake would be nowhere to be found.

Unless, of course, Jake hadn't found a key either, so he'd gone off and left the doors unlocked. Now *there* was a comforting thought, Cassie told herself.

But as soon as she stepped onto the patio she saw movement inside; Jake was in the living room, painting the opposite side of the new door. He looked up when she tapped on the glass and then put down his brush and squeezed past the awkwardly arranged sawhorses in order to let her in.

Cassie told herself that the spurt of gladness she'd felt on seeing him was nothing more than relief; her bag was heavier than usual, and with the crisp breeze picking up, the patio—even sheltered as it was—would not have been an inviting place to sit.

"Thanks," she said. "Do you know the townhouse numbers aren't marked on the back gates? It took me three tries to get the right garden, even though I was trying to count the units. I think I'll go hang a wreath on the fence so I won't get lost next time."

"Why didn't you just come in the front?"

"Because you told me it was going to be sealed off," Cassie reminded. "And it certainly looks as if the draw-bridge is permanently closed."

"It should serve to discourage unwelcome visitors," he agreed. "I thought I was going to have to nail it shut, but eventually I figured out another way."

"First painting, now carpentry. Better watch out, Jake, this handyman stuff might grow on you."

"It is kind of interesting," he admitted. "Maybe if I ever get tired of venture capital, I'll just travel around the country doing odd jobs."

The words echoed oddly in Cassie's head. She bit her

lip and reminded herself that to Jake it was only a casual comment, a throwaway meaningless line, a crazy idea he had no intention of ever acting on. He'd only said it in the first place because she'd teased him.

Nevertheless, he'd said it. *Maybe I'll just travel around the country doing odd jobs.* The phrase sliced through the fog in her brain, allowing her to look at the events of the morning in a slightly different light.

Kissing her like that had annoyed and upset her, there was no question about that. He'd had a nerve to grab her; his behavior had been beyond the pale.

But, in fact, she'd already been unsettled even before Buddy had come on the scene, long before Jake had kissed her—and the subsequent events had overshadowed but not eliminated her original concerns.

What had bothered her this morning—and what was still bothering her now—was the idea that she was nothing more to Jake than a means to an end, a convenient way to speed up his work so he could move on.

Everything came second to that, where Jake was concerned. The idea of staying in motion seemed to be hardwired into his brain.

Even when he was in a joking mood, the one constant about him was that he had no intention of staying in one place. He hadn't just said he'd do odd jobs; he'd had to throw in the idea that those odd jobs would naturally take him all over the country.

Jake was a rolling stone. She'd known that much about him, from what Peggy had told her, long before she'd even met the man. What he'd told her himself confirmed that he had no intention of settling down anywhere or with anyone, no matter how inviting a mossy hollow he happened to run across.

Cassie could hardly claim to be surprised to find that

he was anxious to move on. So why was she so annoyed at him for acting true to form? She should have expected it; she'd had plenty of experience with men who couldn't stay in one place.

In fact, she couldn't count all the towns she had lived in, all the schools she had attended, because her father had always been chasing the next pot of gold, the next rainbow.

But something deep inside her whispered that Jake was different.

Her father had dragged Cassie and her mother from town to town, state to state, job to job. But Jake didn't have a family to drag along, and it was unlikely he'd ever saddle himself with one. And—even more unlike Keith Kerrigan—Jake didn't pretend that the next town, the next state, the next job, would represent permanence. Jake knew exactly what he was doing. He lived in a way he'd deliberately chosen.

Nevertheless, the memory of her father's will-of-the-wisp lifestyle—and of the struggle her mother had made, until she grew too ill, to hold things together and make a home no matter where or for how short a time—created a sudden sick emptiness in the pit of Cassie's stomach that acted on her like a warning shot.

Jake Abbott was tempting, there was no doubt about that. He was full of seductive promise, of easy assurances. But allowing herself to forget that he would never be anything more permanent would be just as dangerous as trusting her father to keep his word and live up to his good intentions.

She was lucky, she told herself, to have that reminder. Not that she really needed it to keep her safe; she was in no danger of falling for Jake Abbott. If Keith Kerrigan had done nothing else for his daughter, he'd served to inoculate her against men of his type.

Cassie's mother had never given up on making friends—and yet she'd died without the comfort of companionship because she'd been too ill to meet anyone in the few months they'd lived in that tiny Indiana town. Cassie, in contrast, had learned almost as soon as she could sing the alphabet that it was easier to keep people at a distance than it was to mourn their loss when it was time to move on. So she'd gone to school, done her lessons, sought solace in music whenever she could find a piano, taken care of her mother and dreamed of the day when she would have a place in the world to call her own.

No, she was in no danger of falling for Jake Abbott. He might not be just like her father, but he was close enough to scare her to death.

Jake said, "Are you feeling all right? You look a little green." He put out a hand as if to feel her forehead.

Trying to act casual, Cassie moved away before he could touch her. "Must be the reflection of the door." She perched on the edge of a chair and dug into the depths of her bag.

"Did you have a chance to talk to the engineer's wife?"

Cassie wasn't fooled by the nonchalant tone of his voice. She nodded, but added quickly, "I didn't find out much. Not what I expected to hear, anyway."

Jake raised one eyebrow inquiringly.

"So call me foolish," Cassie said defensively. "I thought it would be the usual story—that he quit his job because it was too demanding and he wanted to spend more time with his family. Or some variation—maybe he believed things were fine but his wife thought he wasn't devoting enough energy to the family."

"And that wasn't it?"

Cassie shook her head. "If I heard her right, she said he quit because the pace was too slow and the job wasn't demanding enough."

Jake dropped his brush and paint splattered over him. "Damn," he said. "These are my favorite jeans. I don't suppose you'd like to try getting the splotches out?"

Cassie tried to fight off the warm flush that crept up her cheeks. "I'll write down the instructions for you."

"That wouldn't be nearly as much fun as watching you. Sorry, you were telling me...?"

"She didn't seem to be too clear about the details. But the reason he gave her was something about it not being like the old days when the work was exciting, when Caleb was right there in the middle of things and nobody needed to wait for approval and permission before they could act."

Jake picked up his brush again, but the action was almost automatic, as if his thoughts were a thousand miles away.

"Sorry I can't be more helpful," Cassie said. "But I really believe she doesn't quite understand all his reasoning herself." She watched him paint for a few minutes. "I don't suppose Buddy had second thoughts and came back to apologize?"

For a moment she thought he hadn't heard her. "No," Jake said finally. "But he didn't pick up his tools either, so maybe he's thinking it over."

"I wouldn't hold my breath. Especially since you're the one who should probably say you're sorry."

"Now wait a minute, Cassie—"

Cassie ignored him as she dug deep into her bag once more. "When I was at the library today, I found a book I think you should read."

Jake frowned. "I'd have sworn we were talking about Buddy, not books."

"We were. That's what reminded me." Cassie pulled out a big, thick, square book, fully illustrated with color photos, drawings and diagrams. *"The Amateur's Guide to Building Kitchens and Bathrooms,"* she said. "I'd have checked out a book on hanging doors, too, but they didn't have one—I had to settle for a magazine article." She plopped both into his hands.

Jake said, "You don't seriously think *I'm* going to finish up Peggy's bathtub?"

"Why not? You're the one who put Buddy out of the picture. You've got fourteen days before the books are due back at the library, which will be plenty of time."

"By whose definition?"

"Mine," Cassie said firmly. "And yours too, if you're smart, because Peggy will be home in a week. And if the tub's not finished by then and the front door's still boarded up, she'll have killed you long before the books need renewing."

"Maybe I won't be here by then."

Cassie's stomach seemed to drop to her toes. She tried very hard to keep her voice level. "Is the job you're doing for Caleb almost done?"

"Not exactly. But now that you've pointed out the kind of danger I'm in, maybe I should just leave a check and let you explain the details to her."

He wouldn't do it, she reassured herself. He wouldn't actually leave her holding the bag and having to explain it all to Peggy. After all, he hadn't abandoned her with the broken door....

She listened to herself in disbelief. What was the matter with her?

She knew the kind of man he was; he made no secret

of it. She knew if it hadn't been advantageous for him to stay, that he'd have been gone, broken door or not. He'd take his responsibility, of course. He'd pay for the damage he'd done. But it wasn't in Jake's nature to stick around once it wasn't convenient any more, simply to make sure Peggy got the explanation she deserved.

She knew all that, as well as she knew his name—but still her heart had refused to believe that he would go. Despite all the evidence, Cassie had leaped to the conclusion that he would be there no matter what, standing firm and reliable. Next to her.

Because that was where she wanted him to be.

Cassie's head was reeling.

It wasn't fear of facing Peggy that was washing over her right now. It was grief over losing Jake. And that was the most incredibly absurd emotion Cassie had ever experienced. How could she feel sad over losing what she'd never had?

But preposterous or not, the feeling was real. She didn't know exactly when she'd gone over the brink; she only knew she had done so. She didn't know when she'd moved from annoyance to fondness to diffident friendship; it had happened gradually, over a matter of days. The precise timing didn't matter—and it was no more important for her to figure out at exactly which moment she'd taken the next step, from liking Jake to loving him.

Loving.

It hurt her even to think the word. But she knew that denying the fact wouldn't make it go away.

Just a few minutes ago, she'd congratulated herself that she was in no danger of falling for Jake Abbott. And she'd been right, up to a point—because she *wasn't* in any danger of tumbling into love with him.

But only because she'd already stepped over the cliff.

And now that it was too late to climb back up that slippery slope, what on earth was she going to do about it?

CHAPTER NINE

JAKE was looking at her oddly, Cassie realized, and she lifted her chin a fraction and forced herself to smile at him.

She'd sort it all out later—both her feelings and the reasons behind them—and figure out what to do about this sudden, shocking revelation.

But right now, she told herself firmly, the only thing that mattered was to prevent Jake from realizing what she'd done. If he was to figure out that she'd been idiot enough to fall in love with him, even after he'd made it clear that he wasn't serious about any woman and never intended to be, he'd probably think she had no more intelligence than the toad he'd rescued her from in the bathroom.

And Cassie was inclined to agree with him. What kind of idiot was she?

Later, she thought. She'd have plenty of time to berate herself after she was safely alone. She'd have all the time in the world after Jake was gone....

"Are you sure you're all right?" he asked. "I thought maybe you'd done yourself in by walking all the way around the complex carrying that bag. But now you've been sitting down for a while and you're still looking green."

"I'm fine." She knew her voice was too curt, and she tried to soften her tone and shift the conversation. Perhaps if she asked his opinion on professional matters. "I was just thinking—how would you like to trade the money you owe me for a little business advice?''

His slow smile started in his eyes and sent waves of warmth through her body. ''There are other things I'd rather trade than money,'' he said lazily. ''And other subjects I'd prefer to talk about instead of business, too.'' He put down his brush and came to perch on the arm of the chair where she was sitting. ''And I see, from the enchanting shade of pink you've turned, that you know exactly what I mean.''

Cassie leaned away, but his fingertips moved gently over her hair. Each springy curl acted like a conductor, ferrying the tingle of his touch to her scalp; from there it radiated through her body, making each cell quiver in response. His hand slipped gently along the side of her throat to cup her chin and raise her face to his.

''No,'' she whispered. ''Please don't.''

He shook his head slowly. ''You can't just make this go away, Cassie. Pretending to ignore what we share isn't going to eliminate it.'' His lips brushed hers.

The contact was light as a whisper, but the effect on Cassie was like firecrackers going off along every nerve.

''You know where I stand,'' he said against her lips.

''Oh, yes.'' Her voice cracked. ''I know.''

Jake drew back and looked thoughtfully down at her. ''You mean what happened this morning,'' he said. ''I was clumsy, and I'm sorry. I pushed you—and I scared you. I won't do it again. When you're ready, Cassie....'' He kissed her again, his mouth searching, asking, almost pleading.

It took every ounce of Cassie's self control to keep from kissing him back, when what she wanted most was to pull him down to her, to enjoy this moment and forget about forever.

"You know how much I want you," he whispered.

Want, she noted. Not even *need*. Certainly not *love*.

Those few words should have been all the evidence she required to make up her mind; Jake couldn't have made himself clearer. Nothing had changed. He was offering her a brief fling, no more. And since Cassie could never be satisfied with that, there was only one answer she could give.

And yet confusion roared through her brain. In another few days, he might well be gone. Even if his business dragged out and he stayed longer, in a week at most Peggy and Roger would return. Once Cassie's house-sitting duties were finished, she would go home—and so, even if Jake was still in Denver then, she wouldn't see him any more.

After the next few days, she might not see him again, ever.

She simply couldn't have what she wanted; there was no point in even thinking about things like permanence and commitment and forever, because they were out of the question.

The only remaining consideration was whether to grab for the tiny bit of happiness she could have. She could gather up a few warm memories to cherish after he was gone. Or she could coldly refuse herself the small comforts that could be hers, because she couldn't have everything she wanted.

Put like that, the choice was obvious. So what if Jake thought they were only having a brief affair? What he didn't know wasn't going to hurt him. She could play along with that scenario. She could pretend that she, too, was simply seizing a pleasurable interlude.

And in the next few days—maybe weeks, if she were

lucky—she could store up a lifetime's worth of joy. She could savor every bittersweet instant spent with him.

But what if it all became too much to handle? What if she couldn't keep up the pretense after all? What if Jake were to realize that for her it was much, much more than just a fling?

Would she be risking more than she could bear?

The magazine article made it look easy, implying that installing a new door was as simple as sliding a book off the shelf and replacing it with another title. In fact, Jake thought, it would have been easier to bulldoze the townhouse and start over from the basement up.

He tossed Buddy's screwdriver aside and sat down on one of the contractor's sawhorses to contemplate the problem. The remains of the old door had come down easily enough, though of course that had never been the real difficulty. The hitch lay in removing the old, splintered casing.

He reached for a larger screwdriver and paused midmotion, his attention caught by movement in the living room, where Cassie was bending over to add a log to the fireplace. Her corduroy slacks molded a nicely rounded backside, and he settled onto the sawhorse to enjoy the view.

For a reckless moment he considered calling a halt to his work altogether, if only because without a front door—and with a soft but definite October breeze—she was going to be stoking the fireplace all day. And Cassie on display as she tended a fire—stooping, stretching, reaching—was something he could sit and watch for hours on end.

Of course, he thought, there were even better ideas. For

instance, he could just fling her over his shoulder and carry her upstairs....

He sighed, remembering that in a moment of foolishness he'd made a promise to do nothing of the sort. *I won't push you*, he'd said. And so far, he'd kept his word, though it was increasingly difficult to do so.

He'd been so certain he'd read Cassie correctly. He'd have bet his year-end bonus that even if she continued to try to deny the attraction between them, her own honesty and curiosity would eventually tip the balance.

But it had been a couple of days now, and Cassie was unfailingly polite and even talkative—on subjects of her own choosing. But much as he'd tried to discover one, she hadn't issued so much as a hint that she wanted to share his bed.

He clenched his fists in frustration.

And yet, he thought, she wasn't indifferent to him. There was something about the way she looked at him— a sort of sidelong glance sometimes instead of a straightforward gaze—that gave him hope.

Cassie dusted off her hands and stood up, watching the fire flare brighter for a moment before she came into the foyer. "Aren't you freezing?" she asked. "I'm wearing three sweaters, and you're in your shirtsleeves."

"I'm doing physical work here," Jake pointed out.

"You're showing off your muscles, more likely."

That was a point in his favor, Jake decided. She'd not only noticed the muscles but she'd commented about them carelessly, as if it was a subject she thought of often.

"Is the new casing in?" she asked.

"Not yet. The screws holding the old one are about two feet long and apparently embedded in concrete. I've broken two of Buddy's screwdrivers, and I think I've twisted my shoulder out of the socket. Worst of all, it's not the shoulder I slammed into the door, so now both of them hurt."

She clicked her tongue in what he thought was probably mock sympathy. "As soon as the cookies come out of the oven, I'll bring you one to cheer you up."

"I'm cracking every joint in my body putting up a door," he complained, "and you're baking cookies?"

"I have to do something to stay warm."

Jake saw the exact instant that she realized there was a double meaning—maybe even an unintentional invitation—hidden in her words, and he watched with delight as hot color flooded her face.

"And you don't need to suggest that you have an alternative," Cassie said acidly.

Jake grinned. "Of course not. You so obviously already know what it is that there's no need for me to bother. On the other hand, if you'd like me to give you a demonstration instead of merely reciting the words…"

She sputtered and retreated to the kitchen. With his good spirits restored, Jake picked up the screwdriver and tackled the door frame with renewed energy.

He'd dislodged one rogue screw and was working on a second when Cassie came back with a plate lined with chocolate cookies. She hastily set the plate atop the sawhorse and waved her fingers in the air. "They're still very hot," she explained.

Jake reached for her wrist. "I was taught the best way to treat a burn was with cold water," he said. "And the next best way, if there's no cold water handy…" He put the tips of her fingers into his mouth.

Her entire body quivered, and she tried to pull away.

He shifted his grip and innocently ran the tip of his tongue along her fingers. The pulse point in her wrist was going crazy, he noted. Of course that was no surprise; his blood pressure had climbed to record heights, too.

Cassie said firmly, "You know perfectly well that I am not in need of first aid."

She sounded just a little breathless, Jake thought. Reluctantly, he took her fingers out of his mouth, but he didn't let go of her wrist. "All right," he explained cheerfully. "You said the cookies are too hot to eat, and since I spotted a smear of chocolate on your hand I thought you wouldn't mind if I just nibbled on you instead."

"That's the lamest excuse for a line that I've ever heard."

"I have others," Jake assured her.

"Don't I know it. Would you just knock off the effort to seduce me?"

"I promised not to push you," Jake pointed out. "I didn't promise not to remind you that I'm here—and to point out now and then that I'm still waiting for an answer."

"You've had your answer."

Jake thought that all of a sudden she didn't sound quite as sure of herself. "I'm waiting," he said gently, "for an answer I like."

Cassie gritted her teeth.

Now we're getting somewhere, Jake told himself. He lifted a hand to touch her hair, and the springy curls teased against his palm. He wriggled his fingers deeper into the mass.

Behind him, an amused voice said, "Knock, knock."

Cassie shifted her feet as if she wanted to run. Jake didn't move; he let the weight of his hand draw his fingertips down through the soft curls, and only when he'd finished enjoying the sensation did he turn his head. "Hello, Caleb. I didn't hear your motorcycle."

"No wonder," Caleb observed. "You appear to have other things on your mind. I came over to talk to you, but—"

"I'm going," Cassie said hastily.

"Don't hurry on my account," Caleb said. "I wouldn't be crass enough to make any further comments about Jake's state of mind. I was planning to say it looks like there might be some serious work going on here. In fact, it gives me a headache just looking at it, so—"

"Have a cookie," Cassie said from the hallway. "You'll feel better, and goodness knows Jake doesn't need any more sugar—he's jittery enough as it is."

Caleb selected a perfect confection and disposed of it in a single bite. "You're a lucky man," he said and looked longingly at the plate.

"Go ahead," Jake told him. "You heard me get my orders."

Caleb inspected the array of cookies and ate two more. "You know, Jake, if you're not careful with this Rent-a-Wife stuff, you may find yourself stuck with a long-term lease."

Jake grinned. "Because of a plate of cookies? Perhaps I should point out that I'm not the one who's gobbling them. If you'd like a regular delivery, I'm sure Rent-a-Wife would be happy to oblige."

Caleb didn't answer, but he continued to munch while he contemplated the idea.

Jake turned his attention once more to the recalcitrant screw. "I hope you don't mind if I work while we talk, but it's getting chillier and I think Cassie would like to have a working door before nightfall." He intercepted Caleb's thoughtful look and said, a little more sharply than he intended, "And no, that doesn't mean I'm henpecked. Lay off the whole matrimony question, all right?"

"I didn't even utter the word," Caleb pointed out. "In fact, I'd say it's an interesting problem as to why you have the matter on your mind."

"Because I've been thinking about your workers," Jake said. He was a little startled himself at how glib he sounded, for the retort was as inaccurate as it was prompt; he hadn't—consciously, at least—been thinking anything of the sort.

"I'm sure you can explain that to me."

Jake considered. Now that he'd started this, he'd better be figuring out what he really thought. "You want to keep your people. Right?"

"It's a whole lot more efficient than hiring new ones and getting them used to my way of thinking."

"You're absolutely correct. But if that's what you want to do, it's time to start planning in terms of a maturing staff. For one thing, as these guys get older they aren't going to be able to put in twenty-hour days and sleep under their desks anymore. They may not want to, actually—but even if they try, they'll be too stiff in the morning to work."

"If you're suggesting I put cots beside every desk and workbench…"

"I've heard crazier ideas. No, that's not what I'm suggesting, Caleb. But as time goes on your employees are going to acquire other interests—and other problems—besides Tanner and electronics. Things like families and houses. If you can minimize the stress on them all the way around…"

"So I'll put your Rent-a-Wife to work full time, running errands and keeping everybody in cookies."

Jake glanced at the empty plate and said dryly, "Especially you, right? Actually, that's not a bad start, but I was thinking more in terms of things like gyms, weight rooms, on-staff counselors, activities that involve families...."

Caleb frowned and said slowly, "That's going to take a lot of time to organize and administer."

"Time you won't be able to spend on problem-solving," Jake agreed. "Have you thought about my suggestion? Hiring somebody to take on all the administrative details?"

"Yeah." Caleb sighed. "I have to admit that at first I was pretty burned at the idea of losing my job. Being kicked out of my own company."

Jake tried to conceal his irritation. "That's nothing like what I suggested. You'd be the same keystone you are now. More so, in fact, because projects would move along much faster if they don't have to wait for you to plow through the paperwork before you can look at them. That's what made your engineer quit —the slow process and lack of feedback."

"Really?" Caleb looked intrigued.

"Yeah. I got a hunch, so I called him yesterday and asked."

Sorry, Cassie, he apologized. *But if I tell Caleb right now that it was your spadework that clued me in, he'll go off on the marriage train of thought again, and we won't get anywhere at all.*

"Do you think he'd come back?"

"In a minute—if you were as accessible as you used to be. But that means bringing in somebody to handle the details you hate."

"Somebody like you," Caleb said. "Want the job?"

The capitulation came so abruptly that it took a minute for Jake to hear the rest of Caleb's offer. His jaw dropped. "Me?"

"Why not?" Caleb's tone was careless. "It's your idea.

You could probably dictate the job description off the top of your head. And you've already got a grasp of all the important details about Tanner.''

"I don't know," Jake said slowly. "I've never considered making a change.''

And what Caleb was proposing wasn't just a change, it would be a major upheaval in his life. For one thing, it would mean staying in Denver permanently; concentrating on one firm instead of flitting from company to company; not spending half his time studying the next field, the next product, the next business....

Was the chill which crept down his spine like a slow-melting ice cube one of dread or anticipation? Jake supposed only time would sort that out. Time and serious consideration—for he held far too much respect for Caleb either to jump on the idea or to dismiss it out of hand.

"Well, you think it over and let me know." Caleb reached for a screwdriver. "Now, let's get to work on this door so you can keep Cassie happy.''

Cassie, Jake thought. It would be interesting to hear what she had to say about Caleb's offer.

He smiled wryly. She'd probably point out that if he actually started living somewhere on a permanent basis, he could expand the inventory in his refrigerator. Maybe even put *two* bottles of ketchup on the shelf.

Though the evening was far advanced, the furnace still hadn't quite caught up with the chill which had crept into the townhouse during the hours when the front door had been completely gone. In the living room, the only really comfortable spot in the house, the fire still burned brightly. Jake lay on his stomach directly in front of it, elbows spread wide and hands folded under his chin, staring into the flames.

He didn't even seem to hear Cassie come in. She curled up in a chair near the fire with her legs tucked under her, opened the box of birthday cards she was supposed to be addressing for a client, and started to watch Jake instead.

"One thing about it," she said finally, "the place has been thoroughly aired out."

She wondered for a minute if he'd heard her. "You'll be glad to know I've reconsidered the handyman idea. I don't think I'm cut out for the position."

"The door looks really good, though."

"Not bad for an amateur job, I guess."

"You look tired, Jake. Is your shoulder hurting?"

Slowly, he sought out the sore spots. "Which one are we talking about? If you'd like to give me a massage just to keep the muscles from getting stiff, I wouldn't object."

Cassie knew better. But there was something about him, as he sprawled there on the floor, that was oddly vulnerable. Something that seemed to pull her out of her chair and down beside him.

The firelight reflected on his hair, painting gold highlights into the brown strands. He'd changed his shirt for a thick beige ski sweater, and rather than disturb him to take it off, Cassie worked her fingertips through the loosely knit loops. His skin, flushed from the fire, felt almost hot against her hands as she began to rub the sore muscles.

He sighed and turned his head, resting his cheek against the backs of his hands and closing his eyes.

She sat beside him for a long time, gently rubbing his shoulders, his back. His breathing was slow and steady, as if she'd lulled him to sleep, and though she knew she should stop rather than risk waking him, she couldn't force herself to give up this tiny stretch of time when she could pretend that he belonged to her.

Eventually, though, her own muscles began to ache, and Cassie stopped rubbing and simply sat there beside him, her hands arched and her fingertips pressed against his skin as if she was seeking to brand her fingerprints onto his back.

Foolish, she told herself, and slowly pulled away.

Jake rolled onto his side and propped himself on one elbow. "Pianist's hands," he said lazily. "Strong and sensitive. Thanks." He reached out and ran a fingertip across the tendons in the back of her hand. "You haven't played at all since that first night. Not while I've been around, anyway."

Cassie tried to distract herself from the tremor he was sending through her every nerve by giving him a playful answer. "Considering the damage you did that night because of a simple march, I didn't want to break the news to you that I'm adapting *Macbeth* into grand opera. You'd have probably used your bare hands to chop up Peggy's baby grand for firewood."

Jake grinned. "You know me very well, don't you?" His hand slid slowly up her arm till his palm cupped her cheek. "You're shivering. Is it so frightening, the idea of exploring what we have, Cassie?"

"It's not that," she said. "I'm just chilly."

"Then come down here and let me keep you warm."

She shot a narrow-eyed look at him. "You want things both ways, don't you?"

"Yes, I do." His fingertips teased her eyelashes. "Did you have an affair with him, Cassie—the Shakespeare guy? Is that why you're so reluctant?"

"Stephan? No."

"Not because he didn't try, I'll bet." His hand slipped to the nape of her neck. "If I promise I won't do anything you don't want me to, will you come here?"

There was not a shred of doubt in her mind that he meant it, and that he would keep his promise. Her heart whispered, *He's not really like your father, you know*. She might not always like what Jake told her, but she knew it was the truth, and that was more than she'd ever been able to count on with her father.

She couldn't even remember the number of times that Keith Kerrigan had promised this was the last job change, the last move, the last new school. But Jake was different.

Jake was honesty, not illusion. Jake was reality. Jake wouldn't lie to her. And he wouldn't—deliberately, at least—hurt her.

Cassie was tired of the questions which had circled in her mind for the last two days. She was tired of weighing risks, tired of trying to predict the unpredictable, tired of the fluttery misgivings which accompanied any attempt to sort out what she really wanted. She knew that whatever she did, she'd no doubt suffer regrets; the problem was whether she'd rather regret what she'd done...or what she'd missed out on.

Somewhere deep inside her, she realized, the decision had already been made, for the restless uncertainty she'd come to expect wasn't there.

He held out a hand in invitation, and slowly she stretched out beside him on the deep plush carpet.

It was almost frightening, she thought, how perfectly she fit against his body, with her head tucked on his shoulder and his arm curving round to hold her close. She let herself relax against him, allowed her body to take on the slow rhythm of his breathing. "You've been very pensive tonight," she said finally.

"I was thinking about the next job."

So soon, she thought sadly. *So soon*.

She told herself that she should ask, in a bright and

cheerful tone, where he'd be going next and what he'd be doing. But she was too afraid that her voice would crack and give her away, so she just swallowed hard and said nothing at all.

"But not any more. Cassie, you know how much I want you." Jake shifted his position ever so slightly, and suddenly she was looking up at him, into eyes that had gone so midnight dark that she felt rather than saw the question deep within.

If this short span of time is the only chance we have to be together, he seemed to be asking, *do you really want to let it slip away?*

No, her heart whispered, and she lifted her hand to the back of his neck and drew him down to her, into a languorous dream in which time itself slowed to a surrealistic crawl and the only thing that mattered was the two of them and the delicious, all-consuming hunger that they shared.

Cassie was in the kitchen, laying strips of bacon into a frying pan, when Jake came in. He kissed the back of her neck and said, "I thought maybe you'd want to sleep this morning."

She put down her fork and turned in his arms. "And I thought you might like breakfast in bed." She eyed his dark-blue sports coat and open-necked dress shirt. "Next time maybe I should leave you a note."

"So I'll stay in bed? It would be easier if you just stayed there with me."

She'd wanted to. When Cassie had awakened this morning in his arms, the sunlight had been brighter than ever before, the colors clearer. Energy was pouring through her veins, and every sense was heightened almost to the point of being painful.

But then she had begun thinking how much she wanted this to happen every morning—and she had felt the sting of tears begin. Knowing that if he woke and found her crying, she could not possibly explain, she had slipped carefully from his arms and come downstairs to pull herself together—to put the night's magic behind her and face the reality of the day.

She didn't quite look at him. "Next time I will."

He kissed her again and reached for a mug. "I could get addicted to your coffee."

And to me? she wanted to ask. But she knew better. She picked up the fork again and turned back to the stove. "I don't know how you like your bacon."

"Crisp," he said. "But I don't have much time this morning. I have to catch a plane."

She stopped dead, a strip of bacon dangling from the tines of the fork. He'd said last night that he was thinking about the new job, not that it was pending. Not that it was *today*....

He didn't say it wasn't, either, she reminded herself. *And if there is one thing you knew above all, it's that this idyll had time limits.*

But she hadn't expected the end to be so soon.

She tried to compose herself, so she could smile and act calm, as if her heart hadn't just been sliced in half. But Jake didn't seem to have noticed anything strange about her reaction; he'd reached for the telephone and started to dial.

"Caleb," he said a moment later. "I'll be out of touch for a few days. In fact, I'm on my way back to New York right now. But before I leave, I wanted to talk to you about the job you offered me yesterday."

Cassie's eyes widened. He'd gotten a job offer? From

Caleb? But surely that would mean a position at Tanner. And that meant...

I'm thinking about the next job, he'd said. Was it possible that job would be in Denver? Was it possible that the rolling stone had decided to nestle down in a mossy hollow after all? And if he was going to stay...

"It's intriguing," Jake said. "In fact, it's a great offer. But I hope you'll understand when I tell you I can't take it, Caleb."

Cassie felt as if she'd taken a punch to the stomach.

"No," Jake said. "I'm sure. It's not the job for me."

She stared at the frying pan, but she didn't even see the bacon sputter, turn brown, then start to blacken along the edges.

Nothing's changed, Cassie told herself desperately. She'd known he was leaving; she'd accepted the fact and made her peace with it. The fact that he'd gotten a job offer didn't matter a bit. The fact that he'd rejected it didn't make the underlying situation a whit different.

And yet, so deep inside that she hadn't even suspected it herself, she had kept on hoping that something magical would happen, that he would change, that he would realize she was more important to him than his peripatetic lifestyle. At some level she had convinced herself that he would be leaving not because he wanted to, but because there was no alternative. If he'd had a choice, the insidious little refrain went on, he'd have chosen her....

But the fact was, he did have a choice—and he'd made it.

And he hadn't chosen Cassie.

Smoke started to rise from the pan, stinging her eyes.

Great, she thought. *At least I'll have a good excuse for crying*.

CHAPTER TEN

EVEN after he broke the connection, Jake stood for a long moment with the phone in his hand, wondering why it had been so difficult to say no. Before Caleb had made that offer yesterday, if someone had asked Jake whether he wanted to stay in Denver, or whether he wanted to seek a different kind of work, he'd have laughed at the idea.

Yet, there was something very appealing about the offer. He wasn't certain exactly what the attraction was. It might be the chance to nurture a single product all the way from inception to market, and then to point at the result with pride. It might be the opportunity to put his own theories and philosophies—developed in piecemeal fashion at companies all over the continent—to work. Or maybe he was just getting tired of stacking up frequent-flier miles.

Hell, he didn't know. And it didn't matter, because he'd made the only decision he could. He'd turned the question to every angle he could think of last night in front of the fire. And when he'd awakened this morning, he'd known the answer he must make.

The smell of burning meat assailed him, and he dropped the phone back into its cradle and swung around to see smoke billowing from Cassie's frying pan. "What in the...?"

She stared through him almost blindly.

Obviously, it was no time for conversation. Briskly, Jake set her out of the way, seized the pan full of bubbling, blackening bacon grease, and flung the whole mess into the sink, where it sizzled and sputtered for another half minute.

"Not quite that crisp," Jake said.

Cassie didn't smile. She reached for a dishcloth and began to mop up the spatters on the stove top.

"You're upset," he said.

"Of course not. What right do I have to be upset at anything you do?"

The denial annoyed him, because the tightness in her voice told him it was patently untrue. "You're furious that I didn't tell you earlier that I was leaving."

She shook her head. "Just please don't expect me to believe you didn't know till this very minute that you had a plane to catch."

"That's just about the truth. As I was thinking everything through this morning, I realized that I have all the data I need now, and I don't want to waste time presenting it. If I can make that morning plane..."

Cassie looked at him for a long moment, and then shook her head. "You know, Jake," she said, sounding almost sad, "I really thought you were different."

He frowned. "Different from what? The creep who stole your hard work? You can't think—"

"No. But then I thought he was different, too—different from my father. And he was, actually, in a lot of ways. He was stable, settled, reliable—all the things I was looking for. Only those things didn't matter, because he was a user too, and a liar. Like my father." She looked him squarely in the eyes. "Like you, Jake."

He didn't know whether he was angry or wounded. "Cassie, I never lied to you."

"Not to me, Jake. To yourself. You're no more able to see yourself clearly than my father was." She wrung out the dishcloth and blindly wiped at the countertop. "Every time we moved, he swore it would be the last. This would be the perfect town, the perfect job, the perfect situation. But even before we were completely settled, the next opportunity would come along, and he'd toss everything aside because *it* was going to be the perfect job, the perfect situation. And once more he'd swear it was the last time." Her voice trailed off as if her throat was hurting.

"I don't see the correlation, Cassie."

"Of course you don't. And you're partly right—you're not exactly like him. He at least pretended to settle down, even though he couldn't stick with anything for more than a few months. You can't even bring yourself to do that. You got what you wanted last night, and now you're so afraid I'll want more that you're running away."

"Dammit, Cassie—"

"Or maybe I'm not even that important. Maybe it's not me at all. Perhaps Caleb's offer frightened you so badly you can't wait to get on a plane. A job that would require you to stay in one place—what a horrible thought!"

"That's not true," he said. "I'm not running from you, and I'm not running from Caleb's offer, it's just impossible for me to take it."

"Impossible?" she mused. "What a shame, because I'm sure you'd love to settle down. Buy a house. Plant a rose garden. Run for city council."

None of those things had occurred to him, he had to admit, but the mocking note in her voice added fuel to his irritation. "What's so incredible about the idea that I might want to do those things? I've sort of enjoyed the handyman lifestyle this week—even with the frustrations of the door."

"Sure you have, Jake. Have a good trip." She tossed the dishcloth into the sink and walked out.

His fury fizzled like a punctured balloon, leaving only puzzlement behind. What was wrong with the woman?

He followed her down the hall, but just as he set a foot on the bottom step he heard a lock click upstairs.

That seems to be that, he thought. Caleb had been right, after all; this Rent-a-Wife business wasn't all it was cracked up to be. The idea had been great—a way to have all the convenience of someone waiting at home and holding down the fort, without having to check in regularly or answer questions or justify one's actions or decisions. But it hadn't worked out that way at all.

He'd be glad to get home, he decided. Home, musty home, she'd said, and she was right. There was one thing to be said for his apartment, however—though there might be nothing but olives and ketchup in the refrigerator, there also wouldn't be a supposedly self-sufficient woman needing a cell phone torn apart or a door put back together....

Of course, neither would there be a wide-eyed redhead to offer to heat up a microwave hot pack to make a sore shoulder feel better. Or to brew the best coffee on the face of the earth. Or to shyly and generously invite him to her bed. Or to make him feel like a hero for simply rescuing her from a footloose toad...

You're starting to sound like a sentimental slob, Abbott, he told himself. *And for what*? After the way she'd berated him just now...

He checked his watch and picked up the garment bag he'd left in the hallway earlier. By the time he returned the rental car, checked in at the airport, and picked up his ticket, they'd be calling his flight.

He pulled open the front door just as Buddy raised a finger to the bell, and for a few seconds they simply looked at each other, taking stock. "I see you found somebody to fix the door," Buddy said finally.

Jake nodded. "I put it in myself. The job gave me a whole new respect for your skills."

"Did it, now." Buddy didn't smile. "I came to pick up my tools."

"I'd like to talk you into reconsidering that decision. Oh, by the way, I owe you for a couple of screwdrivers."

"You want me to stick around and finish the job instead? Any particular reason I should? And if you tell me it's because you want your shower back—sorry, fella. I'm not interested."

"Besides the fact that you entered into a contract," Jake said deliberately, "I want you to finish the job because it would please Cassie. And also because it will save her a whole lot of trouble if the tub's done when the owner of the townhouse gets home."

Buddy frowned. "The owner?"

Encouraged, Jake took a deep breath and plunged. The explanation sounded, even to his own ears, as hopelessly muddled as a foreign film without benefit of subtitles.

Buddy simply listened, imperturbable and unblinking. Whether he understood was an open question; the only sign of life he displayed was the toothpick which he shifted back and forth across his mouth as Jake talked.

Unsure whether he was making headway, Jake paused to take a breath.

Buddy spit out the toothpick and said, "Honest to goodness?" He sounded younger than ever.

Jake nodded, relieved. "Despite the evidence you think you saw, Cassie's never been in any danger from me. We've had our disagreements, but I hold her in a great deal of respect." His eyes narrowed. "By the way, I expect, if you agree to finish this job, that she isn't going to be in any danger from you either—or else you'll find out what it feels like to be thrown through a wall, not just an already-broken door.''

"Got it bad for her, don't you?" Buddy said casually. "Well, as long as it makes such a difference to her—yeah, I'll finish the job. I've got nothing but time this week."

"Good." Jake held out a hand. "No hard feelings?"

"I wouldn't go quite that far," Buddy drawled. "Personally, I hope she stomps you in the mud. Now, if you don't mind, I'll get to work."

At the top of the stairs, Buddy went into the master suite and Jake gritted his teeth and knocked on the locked bathroom door. "Cassie?"

"Aren't you gone yet?"

"I need to talk to you."

He thought she was going to ignore him, but long seconds later the door opened.

She'd been brushing her hair, and it was wilder and even more inviting than he'd ever seen it before. As if his hand had a mind of its own, he found himself reaching out to touch the mass of curls.

She leaned back, out of reach, her arms folded across the front of a silky blouse, the hairbrush still dangling from one hand as if she half-expected to need a weapon. "Talk," she said pointedly.

Suddenly, Jake felt as if a set of gears had shifted somewhere deep in his brain, and with the blinding force of a migraine headache, he realized what he'd done.

Even though he hadn't taken time to really think about it, he'd been a bit baffled all week by how much he was enjoying himself, just puttering around the townhouse. Now he knew why. It wasn't the house that was the attraction, and he certainly could have done without the challenge presented by the door.

It was Cassie who had created the magic.

Only Cassie.

How could he have missed something so glaringly obvious?

Yes, he'd wanted her. He'd probably started wanting her the first night, when he'd burst through the door to see her sitting at Peggy's piano, modest, innocent, altogether desirable.

But then he'd kissed her, just to prove a point, and he'd ended up with his head spinning so hard he hadn't even stopped to consider what was really going on. He'd thought it was nothing more than wanting. So he hadn't paid any attention when he went all the way past wanting, to needing. To loving...

Whatever gears had shifted in his brain seemed to have disconnected his tongue. That was just as well, he thought. He could hardly blurt out this sudden revelation. Cassie would probably spit in his face if, just a few minutes after he'd cheerfully told her that he'd enjoyed the handyman lifestyle, he admitted that he'd sort of made a mistake about the relative importance of paintbrushes, screwdrivers, and her.

Cassie was watching him intently. Finally she rolled her eyes and said, "Let me help you out, or we'll be here all day. Did I hear two voices in the foyer a little while ago? Two people coming up the stairs?"

"Yeah," he said. His voice was a little gruff, but it would do. "Buddy's back, and he's going to finish the tub."

"Why?" she asked crisply.

"Look, I'm sorry if you don't like the idea of having him working here after what he did—but he's really the only alternative if the tub's going to be done on time." He paused, and added, feeling awkward, "I've made it clear to him that he'd better not create any more problems for you or he'll be answering to me."

"How thoughtful of you," she mused. "And how delightfully macho. Does he know you'll have to deal with him all the way from Manhattan?"

"I'm not going away forever, Cassie. I'll be back in a couple of days." He took a step forward and slipped an arm around her shoulders. "And then we can sort this all out."

She didn't try to avoid him, but she was stiff and unresponsive in his arms.

"Cassie?" He tilted her face up to his.

She looked him straight in the eyes and said, almost gently, "You don't get it, do you, Jake? I'm not going to be your gal in Denver, on call for whenever you happen to land here for a week or two." She pushed his hand away and crossed the hall to the guest room.

Jake followed. "This isn't finished, Cassie. You can't make love with me as you did last night and then dismiss me as if it was nothing."

"Last night was a big mistake. The whole thing's been a mistake. In fact..." she looked up at him appraisingly. "You know, I've just realized that I should have taken your advice a long time ago."

"What advice?" he asked irritably.

She smiled just a little. "I should have left you alone and kissed the toad."

Jake had said it was impossible for him to take the job Caleb had offered him at Tanner Electronics. An interesting choice of words, Cassie thought bitterly, but the answer came as no real surprise.

So much for giving him credit for honesty. She had to admit, though, that she was just as glad that he hadn't spelled out the precise truth behind his refusal. It was bad enough to know it in her heart, but if he'd actually come straight out and told her that she wasn't important enough to him to make him settle down, even when he was offered the chance....

No, she decided. Even that couldn't have been any more devastating than the realization that she'd fallen in love with a man who was every bit as much a user as Stephan had been. A man who was just as blithely unaware as Keith Kerrigan of the damage he was doing. A man who was as incapable as both of them at being straightforward with himself.

Cassie didn't want to count the days, and she was furious at herself for noticing when there was no sign of Jake's return. Hadn't she learned anything from her father's glib promises? Jake had said he'd be back in a couple of days—and more fool she, she'd actually believed him. But two days, and then four, came and went with not only no Jake, but no phone call and no word.

And you're surprised, she gibed at herself. *What a fool you are*!

She was sitting at the grand piano late one afternoon—not playing, only thinking of that first night and trying not to cry —when Buddy sought her out for the first time since he'd come back to work.

He stood in the arched doorway, fidgeting with his leather tool belt. Whatever Jake had told him, Cassie thought, it certainly had been effective; he'd hardly looked at her in days.

"Ma'am?" he said. "I'm done."

"You're quitting for the day? Thanks for letting me know, Buddy. Same time tomorrow?"

"No, I mean I'm all finished—with the whole job. I thought you'd like to inspect it before I go. I've still got some tools to take out to the truck, but then I'll be out of your way."

"Of course." She closed the piano and went upstairs.

The master bath smelled of new construction—raw wood, adhesives, harsh cleansers—and the area surrounding the tub looked pathetically bare, more like a warehouse display than a real room. Peggy would have a hundred decorating decisions to make, from wall coverings to accessories, but Buddy was right; his work was done.

And so was Cassie's. She'd agreed to stay till the tub was completed or till Peggy got home, and now she was free.

While Buddy carried out his tools, she wiped away the haze of dust from mirrors and countertops and replaced all the knickknacks, toothbrushes and baskets of cosmetics which she'd stored in the closet the day Buddy had started to work. She rinsed the new tub and dug out some bright-hued towels to hang on the new racks as a spot of color against the stark white walls, filled a brass bowl with potpourri and set out a scented candle.

The contractor was rolling up his last extension cord when she finished. "Buddy," she said suddenly. "Whatever it was Jake told you that day..."

Buddy shrugged. "He was just staking his claim, ma'am. And I can't blame him for that."

Staking his claim. What a joke that was, Cassie thought.

"If you ever need any plumbing done..."

"I'll call you, Buddy."

He dug a fresh toothpick out of his shirt pocket, stuck it jauntily into his mouth, and carried the last load of tools down to his truck.

Cassie vacuumed the bedrooms, changed the sheets, threw a load of towels into the washer. It was all necessary work, but she couldn't deny that every chore she added to her list gave her a reason to stay a few minutes longer.

Which was really crazy, she told herself. Why did she even want to hang around longer? Was it simply the off chance that Jake might show up?

Regardless of what he'd said, it was apparent that he wasn't going to come back, and in any case there was nothing left to say. To linger in the townhouse was to pretend that the idyll might not be over—and she was finished with pretending.

So Cassie packed up her clothes and put the spare key back into its accustomed spot. It was time to go home.

When Jake rang the bell, there was no answer and no indication of life in the townhouse—only the impassive, unblinking eye of the camera he'd installed above the door. But did that mean Cassie wasn't there, he wondered, or that she had caught a glimpse of the monitor and decided not to face him?

No, he thought, she wouldn't hide. In their last encounter, she hadn't hesitated to compare him to a toad, so why would she bother to avoid him now?

As an afterthought, he checked under the pot of shaggy yellow flowers. At first, when he saw the key lying there, exactly as Peggy and Roger always kept it, he almost didn't believe his eyes.

She's gone, he thought.

The knowledge hit him like a sledge hammer, even though he knew it was stupid to think that nothing would have changed. He'd been away for days. How foolish could he be, expecting that she'd be there waiting for him, when she'd said herself that it was over?

He stood on the step, turning the key over and over in his palm, and debated whether he should even go inside.

Could he bear to face the empty silence? Did he want to look in the refrigerator, where he'd bet his untouched six-pack, two jars of olives, and bottle of ketchup would be lined up with military precision? Or walk past the bathroom, which no doubt—even if she'd been gone for days—still smelled of lilacs? Of course, he could run the security videotape back, just to get a glimpse of her leaving....

You've got it bad, Buddy had told him, and Jake admitted that the man had been absolutely right.

He picked up the key. He'd go straight to the telephone book and look up Rent-a-Wife. He certainly wasn't going to give up now.

The roar of the vacuum cleaner died as Cassie flipped the switch, and she bent to unplug it and wrap up the cord. The living-room carpet had been the last item on her list, and now she thought every trace of her occupation had been wiped away. Peggy would come home to a townhouse that was both cleaner and neater than the one she'd left.

She wheeled the vacuum into the foyer, intending to put it away in the hall closet, just as she heard the unmistakable click of a key in the front-door lock.

Great, she thought ironically. Wasn't that just her luck, that Peggy and Roger would come home early, before she could make her escape? No doubt they'd want a complete report, and she'd have to smile and pretend that everything had been calm and ordinary....

The door swung wide. "Jake," she said under her breath, and could have bitten off her tongue.

He stood absolutely still, just inside the door, and stared from her suitcases piled at the foot of the stairs to her, his dark eyes incredulous. "I thought you'd gone."

Cassie didn't bother to try to keep the sarcasm out of her voice. "No doubt that's why you felt it was safe to come in. Never mind, I was just on my way out."

"But the key was—"

"I put it back so I wouldn't forget at the last minute. If you'll excuse me—"

He stepped into her path. "No, Cassie. I said we were going to sort this out."

"And you also said you'd be back in a couple of days. Sorry, Jake, time's up."

He didn't move. "What are you afraid of? And don't bother to tell me you're not. If you weren't scared, you wouldn't try to run away."

"At least, that's the opinion of someone who's an expert at running away," Cassie countered. "I don't happen to think I'm running, I just don't think there's anything to talk about. But if you insist, I suppose I can give you a few minutes." With a mock-gracious gesture, she ushered him into the living room.

She perched on the edge of an oversized chair; Jake stood in front of the fireplace as if he was too agitated to sit.

"I expected by now you'd be off on another assignment," Cassie said. "Or do you even know where you'll be?"

"Fairbanks, Alaska, is next on the schedule."

Despite everything, Cassie realized, right up to that moment she'd still nourished a flicker of hope. But he'd smashed it as firmly as if he'd set a foot on her heart.

"I don't want to go," he said.

She told herself it was futile to try to read hidden meanings into a conversation when the surface ones were perfectly sensible. She shrugged. "I can't imagine *anyone* wanting to go to Alaska when it's coming up on the short-est days of the year. Congratulations on your good taste.''

"It's not just Alaska, Cassie. It's any place. I sat in the prep meetings, but I just didn't care about Fairbanks, or anywhere else. Too many things have changed in the last few weeks.''

"You liked working on the door that much, did you?''

"You're determined not to make this easy, aren't you?''

"Any reason why I should give you a break?''

"No, there isn't. After I as much as told you that you weren't important to me—''

She raised her chin. "Why should I think I ought to be important? You're far too busy and—''

"Dammit, Cassie, stop pretending to be an icicle! You must care how I feel about you.''

"Why?'' Cassie asked fiercely.

Jake took a long breath, held it, let it out slowly. "Because I want you to care,'' he said finally. "I didn't lie to you, Cassie. At least, I thought I was telling the truth. I didn't know what was happening to me. I grant you, I was a little puzzled about some of the things I was do-ing—and enjoying. But I hadn't stopped to think it through. I didn't know it was you that made the differ-ence, until you told me it was all over. That's when I realized that I didn't just want a quick fling to pass the time in Denver. I wanted—oh, a whole lot more.''

The husky admission should have melted her heart. But Cassie's very bones ached with confusion. He'd said she was important to him, that he wanted more than just an affair. But what did all that really mean? And what was he really asking of her?

He sat on the corner of her chair; though his arms were almost around her, he didn't so much as touch her.

"I'm in love with you, Cassie," he said softly.

I'm in love with you. Her head was spinning. It was everything she would have asked for, and yet....

"And I won't believe that you don't care about me. You wouldn't have made love with me like that if you didn't."

"Curiosity," she said weakly.

Jake shook his head. "You can't expect me to believe that's all it was. But if that's the way you want to play it, all right. Aren't you curious how it would feel to kiss me, now that I'm in love with you?"

He didn't wait for an answer but bent closer to take her lips. Cassie didn't try to avoid him; though he moved slowly, as if to give her the chance to escape, there was something inexorable in his eyes.

And, she admitted, she didn't want to escape. She wanted to be in his arms. In his heart. In his life...

She closed her eyes and tried to surrender, but something deep inside her insisted on holding back. *He's not like your father*, she reminded herself. But would she, like her long-suffering mother, come to regret casting her lot with a man who was so charming, so enchanting, so changeable?

He raised his head. "What is it, Cassie? You're hesitating."

She bit her lip. There was nothing she could do now but take the risk. "Where does this leave me? I'm flattered that you say you love me, but—"

"What would you like me to do, Cassie? How can I prove it? And don't tell me that you don't have an opinion, because I know better. With your background—what you went through with your father—you can't be too wild about the idea of following me around from city to city on this job."

I'd do it, she thought. *I might not like it, but to have you, Jake…If I only knew that the important things wouldn't change, I could handle all the rest.*

"So I won't do that to you," he said. "I won't ask you to follow me."

Her heart sank. "If you're expecting me to be waiting at the airport anytime you can fit in a long layover, let me tell you something, Jake. I'd sooner never see you again than—"

"Oh, you'll see me. I talked to Caleb this week."

"About that job?" She frowned. "I thought you said it was impossible for you to take it."

"It is. There are two reasons, actually. It would be a massive conflict of interest to accept a job offer from a company when I'm in the midst of trying to find venture capital for one of their projects. Doing that would cast a whole lot of doubt on my judgment, my sense of fairness, and my business ethics."

"Oh," she said softly. "I hadn't thought of that."

"You're not the only one. It didn't occur to Caleb, either. Besides, even if I could have accepted it, I wouldn't, because it wouldn't be possible for me to step into a position where I was technically Caleb's boss. He needs to bring in somebody from outside to be his new CEO, somebody who can make a completely fresh start."

Much as Cassie disliked the bottom line, his reasoning all made sense. "Then there's really nothing to talk about, is there?" She wanted to bury her face in his shoulder and howl, but she kept herself upright with sheer determination.

He smiled and kissed her temple. "But now that Caleb's got the funding he needs—which is what kept me in New York all this time—the relationship between us

has changed and there's nothing preventing him from
making me another offer, or me from accepting it.''

Cassie shook her head. ''I won't ask you to do that. If
you wouldn't be happy…''

''I can be happy anywhere you are.''

He was offering her the world—but there was a price
tag attached, and it was one she couldn't pay. Cassie bit
her lip hard. ''Do you have any idea how much that scares
me, Jake? I can't take that responsibility. I can't let you
put so much importance on pleasing me. What if it all
goes wrong?''

''It did for my parents,'' he mused. ''They didn't di-
vorce. It might have been better for all of us if they had.
They stayed together and hated each other instead. That's
why Roger's been married three times—as soon as there's
a disagreement, he takes to his heels.''

''Maybe I should warn Peggy.''

He smiled crookedly. ''My guess is it's too late.''

''The tub?''

''Let's just say if the marriage survives this, maybe
Roger's a changed man. And who am I to say he couldn't?
I have.''

''Jake—''

''Let me finish. I went the opposite direction from my
brother and decided not to take the chance at all. It wasn't
a conscious decision, of course—I just set up my life so
that I never stayed anywhere long enough for anything to
go sour, or get tiresome. Not a job, not a hobby, not a
woman.''

She could hear the strain of disillusioned truth in his
voice, and she could imagine what it had cost him to face
himself.

''You were right, Cassie—I was too busy running to
give myself a chance to ask if it was really what I still

wanted to do. It was only when you slowed me down that I noticed all the things I'd been missing. You're by far the most important of those things. But it wouldn't be truthful to say you're the only one. I don't know everything I want to do. I just know that I want you beside me while I explore all the things I've missed.''

"You're sure?" she whispered. "You said you don't like routine."

"You can't think that working for Caleb will ever fall into a monotonous pattern, can you? And you can underestimate yourself if you want, but I'm not going to make that mistake again. Something tells me I'll be years figuring you out. If you'll let me have the chance."

Slowly the tension seeped out of her body.

"In any case," he said firmly, "I start to work next week as the new chief financial officer and minority partner of Tanner Electronics. So whether you want me around or not, Cassie, I'm going to be here. And since Caleb and I have big ideas of using Rent-a-Wife to help keep his workers happy, you'll have to deal with me. Unless you want to go back and finish school instead."

Cassie considered, and shook her head. "No. I owe Paige and Sabrina too much to walk out on them now. They're my friends—the first real friends I've ever had. And it was true, no matter what you thought—what I told you about discovering that I didn't want to finish my degree. The academic life isn't all ivory towers and poetry, Jake, and I don't want to deal with the back-stabbing and the politics and the pressure. I'd much rather be one-third of Rent-a-Wife."

"In that case, I'll hire you to find me a place to live— but I guarantee I'll be easier to please if you'll promise to move in with me. Because if you don't, I'll just have to keep looking till I wear you down and you change your mind.'' He held her closer; she was trembling and leaning against him for support. ''And I'll be more cooperative yet,'' he whispered against her lips, ''if you'll agree to marry me.''

She kissed him, very slowly.

''In fact,'' Jake said finally, ''if that's a yes, I'll happily live in a cardboard box under a bridge.''

Cassie noted, with detachment, that she seemed to be having trouble breathing, and decided she'd worry about that later; there were much more important things to think about just now.

''I'll start looking tomorrow,'' she whispered, and drew him down to her.

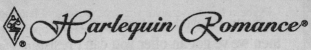

If you enjoyed what you just read,
then we've got an offer you can't resist!

Take 2 bestselling love stories FREE!

Plus get a FREE surprise gift!

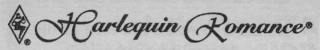

Harlequin Romance®

**On their very special day,
these brides and grooms are determined
the bride should wear white...
which means keeping passion in check!**

WHITE WEDDINGS

True love is worth waiting for...

Enjoy these brand-new stories from
your favorite authors

MATILDA'S WEDDING (HR #3601)
by **Betty Neels**
April 2000

THE FAITHFUL BRIDE
by **Rebecca Winters**
Coming in 2000

Available at your favorite retail outlet, only from

HARLEQUIN®
Makes any time special.™

Return to the charm of the Regency era with

GEORGETTE HEYER,

creator of the modern Regency genre.

Enjoy six romantic collector's editions with forewords by some of today's bestselling romance authors,

Nora Roberts, Mary Jo Putney, Jo Beverley, Mary Balogh, Theresa Medeiros and Kasey Michaels.

Frederica
On sale February 2000

The Nonesuch
On sale March 2000

The Convenient Marriage
On sale April 2000

Cousin Kate
On sale May 2000

The Talisman Ring
On sale June 2000

The Corinthian
On sale July 2000

Available at your favorite retail outlet.

HARLEQUIN®
Makes any time special ™

Visit us at www.romance.net

PHGHGEN